BLESSING AND CURSE

Evanescence Series
Book 3

KAREN D. BRADLEY

Ambrosia Sands Books

This is a work of fiction. All characters and events in this book are purely fictitious, a creation of the author's imagination and any resemblance to actual persons, living or dead, is coincidental.

Blessing and Curse - Evanescence Series

Each book is standalone

Published by:

Ambrosia Sands Books

PO Box 827

Dolton, IL 60419

www.ambrosiasands.com

Blessing and Curse © Copyright 2025 by Karen D. Bradley

Trade Paperback ISBN: 978-1-962714-02-0

Digital ISBN: 978-1-962714-01-3

Cover Art by: Woodson Creative Studios www.woodsoncreativestudio.com

Interior Design by: Lissa Woodson www.macrompg.com

Manufactured and Printed in the United States of America

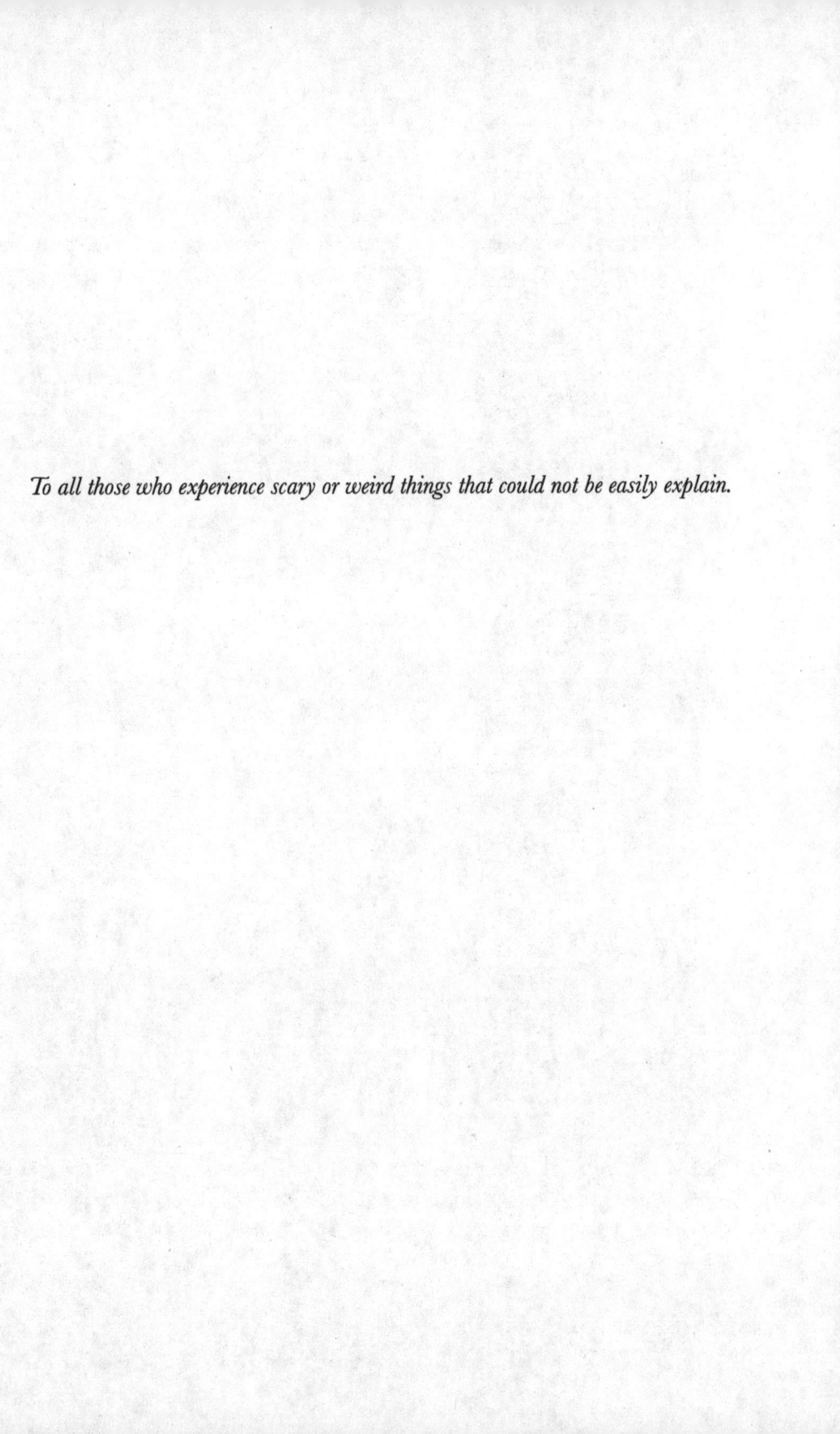

To all those who experience scary or weird things that could not be easily explain.

Acknowledgements

To my family and friends and core group of readers, thanks for supporting me through the ups and downs of this unexpected writing expedition. Most of what I have accomplished has been due to your excitement and encouragement that has provided fuel for a journey.

A special shout out to my sister, Jenetta M. Bradley, for her part in getting my books off the shelf where they were collecting dust. I appreciate you reading my stories repeatedly without complaint.

English and Grammar were never my strongest subjects but the stories in my head didn't seem to care about that fact. Thanks to my editor Lissa Woodson (Naleighna Kai) for your energy and efforts in strengthening the weakness in my writing, challenging me to be better and improving the novel.

To Stephanie M. Freeman and D. J. Mitchell, I appreciate your time and assistance. Your comments, corrections and questions were essential to putting the final touches to the story.

A special thanks to J. L. Woodson for doing what you do best.

Finally, thank you to everyone who purchases a book. Know that your support is appreciated.

Prologue

"We should warn Yolanda."

Khalil stared at the woman with strawberry blonde hair and grey eyes standing behind a guest chair. His eyes returned to the opening in his Castle office wall in Wilmette, Illinois, which was a portal to a block of houses in a Chicago suburb. A woman, with fear coursing through her blue eyes, pulled Yolanda Sunderland into the house.

"Would she believe us if we did?" she responded as Yolanda was escorted through the house.

Khalil moved to his desk and lowered himself into the executive chair. "I thought you said she was an earthbound Tala. Why was there an absence of visions and dreams to tell her she is being targeted by the Fades?"

"Yolanda became one of us by healing a Tala at a young age. It's a transfer that doesn't occur often." She did a swiping motion with her hand, and the image of Yolanda disappeared. "Unlike you, she's not in search of enlightenment as you were when we revealed ourselves to you."

1

"Jalisa, at least give her a guardian." Khalil feared that it might already be too late to save Yolanda from her fate or the Fades.

"She has not been receptive to our attempts." She slid into the guest chair. "The last guardian we sent to protect her nearly died from sulfur powder burns. That chemical has the same poisonous properties as the compound known as Lynxar from our planet, Azurea. "

"The truth is buried within her," Khalil said, as he thought about the story he'd been told regarding Yolanda and eight other individuals attending a dinner. Someone informed her that Fades had found a way to open portals back to Azurea, which could lead to the destruction of Earth. She also received the assignment of protecting the royal family. However, that memory was erased from Yolanda's mind.

"Whatever bits of memories resurface, Yolanda always disregards them as weird dreams," she answered in response to his thoughts.

"We should invite her to stay at the Castle. At least she can be under our watchful eye." Khalil hoped proximity would allow him to slowly introduce her to the idea of the existence of the Tala and Fades and the ancient battle that raged on between the two factions.

Jalisa shook her head. "How do you think she would respond to knowing nine Tala boarded a craft during a war with the Fades and placed their planet in suspended animation? And that the Fades hid among them, then attempted to take over, causing a crash."

"The Fades have set their sights on her."

"They know what she can do and whatever they cannot possess, or bend to their will, they kill." She waves her hand. A small portal opened, showing a van parked on the street of the house Yolanda was visiting. "Today, Yolanda will make a decision that will determine her path."

Khalil looked at the tear in the wall of his office to see three menacing men in a van focused on a set of monitors. The image slowly reduced in size as another opening on the wall grew larger,

2

revealing a muscular man on a queen-size bed with a black comforter partially sliding off the mattress. Seconds later, Yolanda entered the room, and the blue-eyed woman shut the bedroom door behind them.

"Trust the process."

Even though Khalil accepted it was the way it had to be, it did not mean he liked it. Like a diamond, Yolanda's gift and openness to the existence of the Talas and Fades would develop because of the pressure applied to her life. However, it didn't change the fact that it could also kill her.

Chapter 1

Yolanda knelt beside the dying man. Her scalp, which tingled, and heart slammed hard against her ribcage, like a person buried alive and fighting to escape a coffin. His aura had turned murky—a warning which pricked the corner of her mind, a sure sign something wasn't quite right. A faint breeze from his breath warmed her skin as she leaned in close to his mouth. The scent of beer wafted into her nose. Her hands scanned his body, vibrating when they reached the area that most needed healing.

Fear filled Nicole's blue eyes. "You have to save him, Yo-Yo," she pleaded on behalf of her boyfriend.

Yolanda was a psychic surgeon. Not that she would tell anybody, she had the ability to remove disease or operate on body tissue with an energetic incision that healed immediately. Most people wouldn't believe her. Her best friend, Nicole, was one of the few people who knew about this gift. Or, given that she could die healing someone, was it a curse?

"Nikki—"

"Break the rules for me, please." She placed Yolanda's hands on Brandon's chest. "I love him despite his flaws. Please cure him."

Still, she hesitated. Brandon would know too. Dangerous, given the crowd he ran with. Aura colors were important since they reflected a person's personality or mindset. She identified bad people by the ring around their colorful auras. Evil—mentally, and critically ill individuals' auras were full-on murky. Her aunt warned her to only heal people who changed her aura to a green hue. To heal anyone else was a physically draining process. The wrong one could kill her.

Yet, Nicole still believed Brandon wasn't a bad person, but he was friends with men who were known to make money from illegal means and make enemies disappear.

She scanned the room that held a simple oak dresser with a mirror on the wall behind it, a basket of dirty clothes on a chair near the closet, a floor lamp in the corner, and a queen-size bed with a black comforter partially sliding off the mattress and tangled under Brandon's muscular form. She didn't see any voice-activated devices that could potentially record any interaction. The bedroom door was closed. Only three of them were in the room, or so she thought. The reason she made her living as an event planner was to interact with people and, on occasion, have the opportunity to heal someone since the gift nearly overloaded the system when it wasn't used for long periods of time. One would think she'd choose a medical profession, but one fateful visit to a hospital had cured her of that notion. It felt like she had been shot several times and was bleeding out while standing on a live wire. Every muscle was twitching like it was overloaded with a power surge as her internal energy drain made her feel close to death. Weddings, fundraisers, and galas, most folks were too intoxicated to question why she was waving her hands over a guest's body.

"This is a one-time deal, Nikki." She shifted her body closer, unbuttoning his shirt to reveal a pale, muscular chest. "If he ends up in this situation again, I can't help him."

Yolanda could tell he'd ingested the poison by how it filtered through his system. Her hands extended over his chest. Despite her aura not changing to green, she made an energetic incision near his heart, where the poison threatened to do the most damage. The toxin instantly gathered near the incision. Her body weakened as she extracted the contaminant. Silently, she prayed that helping him wouldn't be the death of her. Yolanda fell against the bed, exhausted as the last of the toxic substance seeped from Brandon's system and the ivory skin slid together and sealed as if there hadn't been a large gaping hole seconds before.

Brandon moaned and shifted.

"Baby, you're all right." Nicole plastered herself against his chest as he slowly opened his grey eyes. Her dirty-blond hair slapped him in the face, and he blinked, turning his face away as though looking into her eyes might be too much.

Tears rained down Nicole's cheeks, and Yolanda should have felt a sense of joy, but she couldn't shake the feeling she had made the worst mistake of her life.

Chapter 2

Fatigue threatened to shut down Yolanda's system completely. She couldn't shake the feeling that she needed to get out of the house and put as much distance between her and them.

"Let's get him into bed." Yolanda shifted to her knees and reached for his shoulder and arm, forcing Nicole back so she would take his other side.

A banging noise, as if a door had hit the wall, snatched Yolanda's attention. "What was that?"

Nicole froze. Her gaze snapped toward Yolanda and then shifted away. "I don't hear anything."

She propped Brandon into a seated position, then they struggled to lift him from the floor to the bed.

"Thank you," Brandon mumbled and maneuvered himself into a comfortable position once they hefted him onto the mattress.

When the floor creaked, unease shivered down Yolanda's spine as she asked, "Is anyone else here?"

Nicole shook her head before pressing a kiss on Brandon's forehead, totally blocking Yolanda out.

As Yolanda yanked her purse off the dresser, she caught her

reflection in the mirror. Under the lamplight, her sienna skin was ashen, and dark-brown eyes were dull and bloodshot. She debated whether she felt strong enough to drive home, or if she should catch a rideshare. The urge to leave was so strong.

"Keep him hydrated." She walked toward Nicole with her eyes focused on Brandon. "I'm glad to help, but you can't tell him how I assisted. Come up with a plausible story based on what he thinks happened."

"I trust him." Nicole tugged the hem of her pink tank top lower over her matching sleeping pants while glancing at the bed.

Frowning, Yolanda said, "You trust the people who almost put him six feet under?"

Guilt flickered in Nicole's blue eyes. "I understand what you're saying. I'll try not to give away anything."

That didn't bode well for Yolanda. Her gift was a blessing and a curse. Early experiences had taught her to keep her ability and any odd occurrences top secret. If Nicole had told Brandon anything prior to this incident, she doubted he'd have believed her.

Brandon's "friends" were part of the Russo syndicate, who had built an organization that controlled illegal trade from the streets to corporate offices. She had run afoul of them once before and with a new European faction trying to inch them out of viable territory, the body count was getting higher every day. She could see them trying to monetize her talent for their criminal enterprise. "Let me get going."

The bedroom door flew open, banging against the back wall. A man with rugged features, a buzz cut, and a body that barely fit in the door, locked gazes on Yolanda and smirked.

Nicole gasped and staggered away from the bed. "Adam, what are you doing here?"

"Your girlfriend isn't so crazy after all," said the man who stepped into the room behind Adam, a heavy-set blond with a jagged scar on his jaw. "I thought your story was pure malarkey, but still needed to know if it might be true."

"You poisoned me," Brandon groaned to Gerald, the one who was obviously in charge. He shifted the comforter off his body and attempted to sit.

Yolanda's heart escalated to a rapid pace that outdistanced her breathing. She scanned the room for something she could use as a weapon. Her heart pounded harder. The best weapon, a metal statue, was too close to Gerald. She was trapped.

Adam snatched Nicole by the waist and dragged her across the floor.

Her high-pitched scream filled the room as she flailed against his body.

"Gerald, help me. Don't let him hurt her," Brandon pleaded.

Handling her like a rag doll, he threw her into the closet, then jammed the chair underneath the handle.

Before Yolanda could make a move to the window, Gerald's thick arm snaked around her and he lifted her from the ground. Adrenaline flooded her system and she swung a fist, trying to connect with his face. "We need her for something else." He tightened his hold, dragging her back to the door as he barked an order at Adam. "Remove the cameras. We don't want to leave any evidence."

Nicole screamed and banged on the closet door. "Brandon, you promised. How could you do this?"

"This incident will be our little secret." Adam shoved Brandon hard enough to bounce off the headboard. "No drunken conversations with friends about this." He lifted his jacket and flashed a 9-millimeter.

"Cameras?" Brandon yelped as Adam extracted several small devices off the top of the floor lampshade and crossed the room to snatch another one from the headboard and the mirror.

Gerald frowned. "How else would I know you weren't lying? Figured taking her would be a good way to pay the money you owed us."

Chapter 3

Yolanda fought harder even though she was feeling weak. If murkiness around their aura was any indicator, she would end up a dead woman after they took her out of the house. She stretched for the vase on the side table, but Gerald dragged her through the house and out the back door.

She fought to rip his tattooed hand away from her body. Adam jotted past them and opened the side door of the van parked next to Brandon's sports car. Changing tactics, she grabbed onto the banister as they headed down the stairs.

"Don't make this harder than it needs to be." He yanked her, trying to loosen her hold on the metal.

She waited for him to pull again then released. The force caused him to fall back. Yolanda kneed him in the groin and took off running. Police sirens could be heard in the distance. Yolanda hoped they were coming for her but how would they know? Maybe Nicole had her phone with her and called from the closet. Gerald recovered quicker than expected, blocking her attempt to make it to the front lawn. She changed direction, aiming for the dark alley. Adam jumped from the van, causing Yolanda to pivot toward the neighbor's yard. Gerald tackled her, then set her upright before she could feel the full weight of his body. His fist slammed across her face, then yanked her to his chest.

"Keep it up and I'll have Adam shoot you in the leg." He tightened his hold, dragging her back to the van.

A brown-haired neighbor raced outside with his gun and shot the open ground between Gerald and Adam.

Yolanda used that moment to elbow Gerald in the neck, allowing her to escape. The culprits slowly inched out of the neighbor's yard with hands hovering near their guns.

Chapter 4

Yolanda hated that Nicole's betrayal had forced her to take a leave of absence from work and flee overseas. That night kept playing on repeat in her head. Why hadn't she seen the cameras? A light touch on the arm jarred her from pondering the nightmare that changed her life. Electrical currents shot through her body, but it wasn't due to fear. Her focus returned to where she stood — the Durabian palace's elegant foyer decorated in rich shades of purple and gold. The incident that forced her to leave America, with danger on her heels, was no longer at the forefront of her mind. Despite the betrayal, she'd lived to heal another day. Now, she was captivated by the handsome man standing before her. His olive skin, deep brown eyes, neatly trimmed mustache, and sexy goatee painted an attractive picture.

"I didn't mean to startle you." His voice was deep and husky, reminding her of nights by the fire with a glass of cognac in hand.

She was trying not to freak out in front of a total stranger, but her own aura had never turned red in the presence of another human being. Her soul shivered, then went up in flames as if she had entered a burning building with no escape in sight. The heat coming off her skin made her want to rub her arms. She'd never had such an intense reaction to anyone. Yolanda studied the brilliant crimson glow surrounding him that matched hers measure for measure.

He stepped away from her and his aura turned turquoise, which meant he had a dynamic personality and was a natural organizer. This confused her even more. Her aura only ever turned green or murky in the presence of people who were in need of healing.

Maybe this situation has me losing my mind.

"I am Rashid Ali Khan. I will be escorting you to house-keeping."

Yolanda took offense to his aristocratic tone, which had previously sounded so sensual but now sounded more dismissive.

"Follow me," Rashid commanded with a taut face, before moving toward the main hallway without bothering to see if she had followed.

She didn't know what insulted her more, his condescending tone, or the assumption that she was hired help and not a guest. "I am not a maid."

A tall, curvy American woman with dark-brown hair approached the two of them with long strides. Earlier, Angela Mitchell, who carried a white glow, introduced herself as an employee of Crossroads Security. Angela had been assigned to Yolanda because she was fluent in Arabic.

"Are you sure?" Rashid paused as he looked down at the cell phone in his hand.

Yolanda huffed and crossed her arms across her small breasts. "Why is that your first assumption? Is it because I'm a woman?"

"No, but you may want to watch your tone." Rashid gave her a steely gaze, which she also did not appreciate.

He must be great at organizing things for the palace because his personality is severely lacking.

"You're the one who needs to check your attitude." She pushed down her annoyance at his stuffiness and overbearing demeanor. Heat flushed her neck and she pressed her lips together trying to control the rising anger.

Sexy or not. She would not tolerate rudeness.

Chapter 5

Rashid studied the petite woman, whose soulful, honey-brown eyes radiated anger. Her flushed skin confirmed annoyance as she glared at him.

He should be the one who was annoyed. Jaspar Karim, the Ambassador of Finance, continued to waste his time with requests that kept him from his job as a financial analyst. Rashid suspected his investigation into account discrepancies was the cause. Having only returned from America seven months ago to take this position, he wanted to assure his uncle, Sheikh Kamran, that the appointment wasn't a mistake.

"Clearly, there is a misunderstanding." Rashid retrieved Jasper's email on his cell.

"Hmph." She twisted her full, peach-glossed lips, then muttered, "There's no misunderstanding for the lack of common courtesy."

The new housekeeper was the only person scheduled to arrive at this time. Scrolling down the official daily arrivals list, he saw nothing to conflict with that information. Who was this beauty cutting him to shreds with her eyes? And judging by the fact her hands had curled into fists by her side, he may need to contact the royal guards.

"What is your business at the palace?" he asked, trying not to sound impatient and slightly disturbed that the soft scent of lilac did not escape his senses, nor did her captivating looks.

At the sound of brisk footsteps coming toward them, they both looked in Angel's direction.

"Rashid, I see you've met Yolanda Sunderland," Angela said. "She'll be Daron's guest for a few days."

She glanced at his phone as she reached their side. "She was added to the arrivals list early this morning. Someone should have been emailed you an updated one."

A Durabian woman entered the foyer, escorted by a stocky guard. She had to be the new team employee.

"Enjoy your stay." He nodded, then headed toward the new housekeeper. Glancing back, Rashid realized he should have apologized for mistaking Yolanda for staff and for being curt. His phone buzzed with a fifteen-minute reminder. At this rate, he'd be running late for his meeting with Sheikh Kamran. Apologies would have to come later.

Rashid rubbed his goatee as he pondered a few things. Months of frustration were getting to him. Why did Jaspar ask him to handle such a simple task when someone from the staffing department could have taken care of it? Maybe Jasper was well aware of his appointment with the Sheikh to discuss the discrepancies within the royal accounts.

"Dalia?" He approached the woman, not wanting to make the same mistake twice. His thoughts drifted to the beautiful, feisty Yolanda. What had brought her to the palace at the last minute? Her appearance here without any notice was curious, and the possible reason intrigued him.

The woman in front of him nodded and handed him an envelope.

In Arabic, he instructed, "Follow me." He glanced at the white and silver envelope and was shocked to see his name. "Who gave this to you?" He scanned the area and caught someone shifting into the shadows of the hallway.

"I do not know him," she replied, struggling to keep in time with his long strides. "He gave me that and pointed me in the direction of the guard who led me in."

As Rashid slowed his steps while guiding Dalia to the staff area, he cracked the envelope open and read the note inside. *Stop searching for trouble or you will find it.*

Rashid didn't scare easily. Now, he was more determined to find where that missing money was going. The Sheikh entrusted him with finding out why the treasury suddenly had a fluctuating amount of currency flowing in the wrong direction. An untrained eye would not have made the connection. Thankfully, Sheikh Kamran had made certain Rashid had the skill set for the task.

The moment Rashid entered Sheikh Kamran's office, his gaze went to the Durabian flag in the corner. A sense of pride filled his chest because it reminded him of the strength of his people and the sweeping changes that had been made to the cultural norms.

Daron, the King of Morgan Park and owner of Crossroads Security, wearing a tailored black suit, was seated in an executive guest chair. He was a board member of The Castle, who partnered with Sheikh Kamran and on occasion, provided extra protection to the royal family. Something that became a necessity when Sheikha Ellena was kidnapped by Nadaum royalty and a full-scale rescue mission resulted.

"Let us get down to business." Sheikh Kamran motioned to the empty chair next to Daron. "You found financial discrepancies."

"Yes." Rashid lowered himself onto the seat. "I brought them to Jasper's attention. He told me to look deeper, but I do not feel he believes there is an issue."

"Why are you convinced?" Daron asked, his dark eyes narrowing.

"I received this today." Rashid dropped the unusual envelope onto Kamran's mahogany desk. "The note inside confirmed I am on to something."

Rashid studied his uncle as he scanned the letter. A handsome man with the same dark hair, olive complexion, and neatly trimmed goatee. He ruled the kingdom of Durabia with fairness and wisdom. In an attempt to seize power, Rashid's oldest uncles had turned on Sheikh Kamran and done unforgivable things to take control of Durabia. Rashid was glad his father was the second son of his grandfather's fifth wife. Otherwise, he may also have been caught up in the madness and the unfortunate consequences that befell members of the Khan family who were closer in succession to the throne.

"How did you come to receive this?" Kamran slid the paper under the envelope flap and passed it onto Daron.

Without hesitating, Rashid answered, "The new housekeeper."

"Did you mention it to the royal guard?" Daron asked, scanning the sheet for himself.

"You are the first people to know about this." Rashid retrieved his phone in case he had to show the screenshots he had taken of the discrepancies.

Daron pulled a tablet from the inner pocket of his navy jacket. "I'll review the video to see who was behind the handoff."

"From this moment on, only report findings to me or Daron." Kamran's gaze slid to Daron. "We need Rashid to have a protective team at all times."

"I disagree. Having one would increase the chances of them coming after me." Rashid knew having a security guard around would feed into their enemy's suspicions.

"Let's take a step back and think about it. We can meet tomorrow to discuss the options," Daron suggested.

Rashid was grateful Sheikh Kamran saw the benefit in his observations. No need to bring unnecessary attention and heighten the danger for him and others.

Chapter 6

"Do not open anything from Nicole."

Dread filled Yolanda at her father's words. Her gaze settled on the emails, which included one she had already opened from Nicole when she first landed in Durabia. As a former police officer, he taught her and her mother how to protect themselves. Yolanda sucked in a breath and put the phone to her other ear. "Why?"

"They may use her to track down your location," he explained. She pictured him sitting behind his white oak desk with his bushy brows wrinkled and his reading glasses perched on the edge of his nose.

In the email, Brandon apologized for getting drunk and telling Gerald and Adam what Nicole had let slip about Yolanda having a special gift. He never expected his friend would install cameras, poison him, and attempt to kidnap Yolanda.

Yolanda was relieved they decided she wasn't worth the bullet the neighbor threatened to put in their chests. Or maybe the police sirens sounding as though they were turning on the block was what deterred Gerald and Adam.

"Yo-Yo. You okay?"

21

Her father's voice brought her back to the conversation. She swallowed hard, then said, "Dad, you're a couple of days late and several dollars short."

"Baby girl." He let out an exasperated sigh. "I used my Castle connections for you to lie low, not keep in touch with the person who got you into this situation." His voice held a hint of disappointment, which was like an arrow through her heart.

She padded over the plush rug in the gold and purple sitting area and headed to a set of glass doors leading to the balcony. The desert heat hit her as she stepped out but a faint breeze off the Durabian sea followed. "I had no intention of replying. I was curious to see what she was talking about."

"What did she say?" he huffed.

"Adam harassed her on the job a few times trying to figure out my location. Brandon is no longer associating with Gerald." She wrapped her arms around midriff, though the action provided little comfort. "No one has seen Adam or Gerald in days. She also hasn't been able to reach Brandon."

Daron's team already suspected they were in Durabia.

Yolanda thought her dad was wrong when he shared his suspicions. Now she knew his intel had been spot on.

"You have a new phone for a reason. Don't log into your email or social media until we shut them down." The frustration was clear in his voice. "And please don't contact Aunt Connie or any family members, except me, until we get this handled."

Damn. Her dad must have sensed she was itching to talk with the one person who understood her dilemma. Years ago, Yolanda had called Aunt Connie to escort her to the hospital when Nicole's mother became critically ill. Her aunt, who had a similar gift, taught Yolanda everything she knew about psychic surgery, shared her medical books to study, and passed on knowledge based on years of experience.

Yolanda spent a lot of time with her aunt and uncle and always wanted a love like theirs. They were friends who deeply respected and supported each other. She wished she could say the same about her parents. Her mother loved her father but there were many moments where Yolanda questioned whether she actually liked him. However, it could have been a result of her mom not being completely honest about her gifts. The only reason Yolanda knew about her mother's ability was because of her aunt.

"What about Mom?" Yolanda reentered the room, glancing at the black Abaya that now laid on her bed. While she wasn't required to wear the loose robe-like garment, Angela thought it would make it harder for people to recognize her, especially with the hijab on. Those enemies would need to be close to see her face, plus they probably expected her to be in American clothes.

"No. I'll see if Daron can connect you with Martina Rossi. She also has a gift of healing."

Yolanda's head filled with questions. She wanted to ask Martina how she navigated life with it. Was she born with the gift like Yolanda had been? Or was she like Aunt Connie and developed the gift when she turned eighteen? "Is she here in Durabia?"

"She's a Castle member who resides in Chicago but I'll see if Daron can arrange a video chat."

"Okay, see if Daron can arrange it."

"No calling your mom because she's a leaky pot when it comes to keeping a lid on things," her father said in a quieter voice that made Yolanda think her mother was nearby.

"I understand."

"I'm glad you do," he countered. "Your life depends on it. The police found Brandon shot to death in an abandoned warehouse."

A knock on the door drew her attention. Most likely, one of the security guards.

"Yes." Yolanda moved away from the amazing view her window offered.

She opened the door. A woman stood there wearing a black suit with a Durabian pendant on the lapel and a nametag with Beverly etched into it. Yolanda studied her aura, which was amber with black trim and small particles floating within it.

"I will be your guardian for the day. Angela will escort you to the meet and greet for several new arrivals to the Palace later this evening. You should receive a calendar invite soon." Beverly lowered herself into the chair next to the door.

"Thanks." She stepped out into the hallway.

Beverly shot to her feet and stuck an arm out, blocking her path. "Where are you going?"

Yolanda frowned. "Just getting some fresh air."

"Do you have your bracelet and earrings?"

She pushed back her hair to show the diamond earrings then lifted her arm to show the tactical bracelet. Angela had shown her how to use its features but Yolanda hoped she'd never have to use it.

"Okay." Beverly lowered her arm.

Yolanda moved through the halls towards the exit with her shadow following only steps behind.

"Does Daron really think I need protection on palace grounds?" She asked, locking the phone and accepting the invite before she forgot.

Beverly smiled. "I wouldn't be here if he didn't think it was necessary."

They stepped into the desert heat and Yolanda took in the beauty of the palace grounds. The sound of the Durabian sea in the distance relaxed her. Several men milled about, adding more landscaping to the area. She overheard that it would hide their defense shield being created by Calvin Atwood. The team was in the second phase from what she could gather.

Rashid and Daron exited through a set of doors further away and disappeared behind the hedges. Every time she saw Rashid, she thought about what had happened at their first encounter. She tried to search the various meaning of red because it couldn't be what she thought it was. Red represented aggression, risk taking, power, passion and confidence. She was leaning towards the combination of aggression and confidence being the reason her aura turned red around Rashid. He seemed to have those things in abundance. Enough to overtake her aura. She pulled out her cell, reviewing the list of the meanings again.

"Yo-yo."

Yolanda looked up from the phone and glanced around, listening. She could have sworn she heard Nicole calling her. Then she heard it again. She quickly began following the sound. If they managed to get a recording of Nicole's voice on the grounds, she would need to tell Daron. As she neared a bush, she saw a frog hop into the shrubbery.

"Yo-Yo."

"Are you okay?" Beverly asked as she inched closer.

Glancing back, she debated whether to ask the question. Yolanda hesitated then asked, "Did you hear anything?"

"No. We should probably go back in," Beverly suggested.

"Yo-yo."

Unlocking her phone, Yolanda pulled up the camera app and selected video. "Give me one second." She hit record hoping that she'd hear it again. The frog came out and settled at the edge of the bush.

"Yolanda step back." Beverly moved closer, pausing as someone called out her name. She looked back as if to see who it was.

"Are frogs dangerous here?" Yolanda slipped the phone into her pocket and inched backwards. Instead of moving back, she felt herself being dragged forward. She braced, expecting to hit the bush, but there was no impact. When she stopped moving, she was standing in the Spice Souk with the frog at her feet.

What the hell?

She glanced back to see Beverly at the palace racing to the opening that was getting smaller by the second. "Run! I'm sending help."

Chapter 7

Run.

Beverly's voice seemed to echo in Yolanda's head. Run where? The smell of the various spices filled her nose as she looked around at the numerous vendors. A vendor offered a small group of tourists samples of what Yolanda assumed was tea. She spotted what looked like a street at the end of the row of stores and ran in that direction. Then, she spotted Gerald in the crowd and pivoted in the opposite direction. Heart raced as she flew past people looking at her as if she had lost her mind.

"Crazy American." She heard as she almost knocked over a vendor.

Yolanda had no idea where to go. Every opening she passed seemed to lead to more stores. Could turning down one lead to a dead end? Or would it lead to another aisle of stores? She had no way of knowing. Now, Yolanda wished she had been there before but visiting the Spice Souk with Angela was scheduled for tomorrow. Gerald was closing the distance between them. Yolanda noticed a street ahead of her and aimed for it.

Go left

Yolanda was scared to follow Beverly's voice after thinking she had heard Nicole calling her landed her here. Something deep within said trust it. When she took the left, she glanced back to see a car pull away from the curb. She entered the Gold Souk, passing stores with jewelry, perfume and clothing.

Hide.

She ducked behind a rack of clothes and Gerald raced past. When he was further down the street, she moved from her hiding spot. A child broke free of his mother and knocked the perfume bottle from her hand. It crashed to the pavement causing everyone nearby to look their direction, including Gerald. He raced in her direction as she maneuvered through the crowd trying to reach the road. Yolanda turned right onto the street.

Don't go that way.

The warning was too late. Seconds later, Yolanda was being snatched off her feet and thrown into the back of a car. Adam quickly secured her hands with a zip tie and then wrapped a scarf around her mouth.

The driver pulled off then picked Gerald up. Adam tapped the driver's shoulder. "Cuz. You were right."

He looked back and Yolanda could have sworn she saw something move horizontally over his eyes. It reminded her of a nictitating membrane she'd seen on some reptiles.

What the hell?

The driver's aura was murky but he seemed to have small particles floating in it. She had only seen that a few times but hadn't gotten around to asking her aunt about it.

Her heartbeat increased as she made sure she could reach her bracelet. At the right moment, she would try to cut through the ties. They drove a few minutes before they dragged her out of the car into a building.

"Dad, we found her." Adam shoved her towards an old man in a hospital bed with a cannula pushing oxygen into his nasal passage.

This had to be Zander Busch. Daron had said he's second in command of the Russo syndicate and Adam and Gerald's father.

"I'll prepare to dispose of her body?" The driver said as Adam settled her in a chair next to their father.

Both Adam and Gerald looked at him. "What?"

"She has not yet accepted her partner and hasn't come into her full power. This will likely kill her."

Yolanda knew she could die but she had no idea what he meant by she hadn't fully realized her gift. Her aunt had warned there would come a point where she could heal people without potentially losing her life. Maybe that was what he was speaking about.

"We need to do it in sessions." Adam retrieved a pocket knife and lifted her from the chair by the arm.

Gerald pulled out a gun and aimed at her as Adam sliced through her ties. "He has lung cancer, pulmonary hypertension, and his kidneys are failing. Can you target a specific area?"

"Yes." Yolanda squeezed the tracking earring, praying that the Crossroad Security team would make it to her soon. The father's organs seemed to be shutting down on him. She hesitated, debating her options. Yolanda questioned if they would kill her if she said no. She didn't think so. "I won't do it."

The cousin lifted a Glock. "You will definitely die now if you don't heal him."

A chill went down her spine as he gave her an evil smirk. She took a breath and focused on the older man. The dark murky aura around him made Yolanda say a silent prayer as she hovered her hands over his heart. She figured it was her best bet because they would need to see the improvement without any medical testing. The longer her hands were over of him, the weaker she felt.

"His pulse is improving." Adam stared at the machine next to the bed, eyes widened with shock.

"Catch her."

Those were the last words she heard before crashing to the floor.

⊏⊐

HER EYES FLUTTERED OPEN SOMETIME LATER. She didn't know how much time had passed. Her arms were bound behind her back. Yolanda used one hand to turn the bracelet to reach the circular metal piece in the center. When she flipped up the circular piece, the knife on its underbelly was revealed. She carefully slid the zip tie near the blade then tried to press the metal circle down. It took several tries, but it finally sliced through the plastic.

She stood still, feeling a little wobbly. The small room only had a dirty window, which didn't provide any view of the outside, and the piece of mattress she had been on. Yolanda moved to the door and listened for voices before trying to turn the knob. She had hoped that they had left it unlocked, secure in the fact that she was tied up. No such luck. She went to the window and took the bracelet off and pressed the knob on the clasp to reveal the piece that could break windows. Yolanda tore pieces of her shirt, wrapping them around her hands. She'd only have seconds after breaking the glass to get out.

Wait.

Yolanda glanced back as if she would see Beverly. The knob rattling, she decided that despite the voice giving her good directions before, waiting didn't sound like it. She slammed the bracelet against the window panel. The glass shattered as the door flew open.

"You're safe," Angela called out as Yolanda reached for the window ledge.

She rushed towards the door, wanting to get out before the Russo crew attempted to stop them. Yolanda followed Angela past the room where the elder Busch was stretched out in front of Gerald, who was tied and gagged in the chair. One thing Yolanda knew was that if they captured her again, they would not allow her to do sessions. Healing him would be certain death.

29

Chapter 8

Rashid noticed Yolanda the moment he'd followed Daron out of the palace. His thoughts had drifted to her several times since they met. His investigation of the finances needed to be his focus instead of thinking about what brought her here. He was glad she'd be leaving soon and he wouldn't see her around the palace. He wondered if her significant other would be joining her

"We're here," Daron said, interrupting Rashid's thoughts.

He hadn't even been paying attention to where Daron was leading him. Daron opened a door hidden by shrubbery. Rashid felt the energy as he entered the private room, which had a couch, two chairs and a coffee table in front of the one wall that was a screen.

"What is this about?" Rashid followed past the bar setup to the seating area.

"Khalil Germaine wants to have a private word with you." Daron picked up a black remote on the table, hit the button and exited the room.

"Rashid, have a seat."

He glanced at the screen wall to see Khalil sitting behind a desk.

"Has Sheikh Kamran informed you of my suspicion?" Rashid lowered himself in the swivel chair and shifted it toward the screen.

"Yes, but I want you to understand that there is a fight in the palace between good and evil. That you need to accept and understand that pursuing this makes you a target." Khalil leaned forward, staring at him as if he was trying to see into his soul. "This is as much of a spiritual warfare as it is physical."

"I understand." Rashid hoped this made his uncle realize he's not like the family that had turned against him and was trying to undermine him.

"Remember that you can reach out to any of the Kings or Knights that they are in Durabia to assist you." Khalil turned back, looking at a strawberry blonde woman in the background. She nodded and Khalil returned his focus to him.

Rashid tried not to let his confusion show on his face. Why was this woman in the room during such a private conversation? "I know, but we have to be discreet not to show our hands."

"I have to go, but remember you're not in this alone."

Khalil stood and the screen went black. Daron entered seconds later and pulled a velvet sack from his pocket.

Rashid stood. "What is that?"

"Khalil decided that if you were going forward with this investigation, you'd need a tracker." Daron handed him the pouch. "I thought a watch is more your style than earrings or a tattoo. Plus, it has some additional features." He showed Rashid how to navigate the different aspects of the watch.

"Thank you." Rashid smiled, knowing this technology would help him greatly with his search for the truth.

"If you're in trouble, just press the Durabain emblem." Daron walked towards the door.

"What if I am not in a position to?" Rashid took his old watch off and placed the new one onto his wrist.

"We'll activate it for you." Daron led him to Sheikh Kamran's office and his staff escorted them in.

"Rashid, I know you don't want it but you need a protection team." Sheikh Kamran stood glancing out the window then glanced back at Rashid.

"If you do that, I can no longer covertly search for the problems," Rashid argued. Having assigned personal guards when they were usually stationed in discreet areas when he was outside the palace grounds would be a red flag. The culprit would know he hadn't ended his efforts, and Rashid had no intention of abandoning the job. This was his opportunity to prove himself and solidify his position. Kamran had divided Durabia into districts and the goal was to eventually oversee the financial one, but he had to earn the Sheikh's trust and respect. Especially since so many had failed him.

"I have an idea. Yolanda requires twenty-four-hour protection. We were planning to move her into an apartment in the free zone at the end of the week," Daron stated, referring to the area of Durabia where the laws weren't so strictly enforced, and the traditional mindset did not dominate.

"You plan to have her remain in the palace instead?" Kamran leaned forward and rested his elbows on the desktop.

"We can post a second guard outside Yolanda's room. It allows us to watch over Rashid when he's most vulnerable," Daron explained, typing into his cellphone.

"Her room is right down the hall from the one you stay in when you are here." Kamran turned toward his laptop and his fingers flew over the keys. "You and Yolanda will become the Outreach Gala committee."

"Uncle, I do not..." Rashid grimaced, trying to come up with a valid argument to get out of an assignment that would put in close proximity to a woman who seemed to despise him. He also did not want such a beautiful distraction near him every day`

"Either work with her or you will have your own protection team." Kamran's steely gaze let Rashid know they had reached the nonnegotiable stage of the process.

Rashid only had one main suspect. If others were involved, they could start covering their tracks. He wanted them to believe that their threats had worked. "Let me know how this project with Yolanda is supposed to work without interfering with my investigation."

Daron pulled out his cell, glanced at the screen and stood. "I need to take this."

Rashid looked at his uncle. "It must be important if he took a call while in a meeting with you?"

Daron rushed back into the office. "I have a situation I need to monitor. I'll work out the security details with Rashid a little later." He was back out the door before anyone could respond.

Rashid looked at his uncle. "Is everything okay?"

"If his swift exit is any indicator, I would say no." Kamran came and stood next to his chair. "But that is why I want his team to watch over you. I know that will stop what they are doing and battle whatever obstacles necessary to keep you safe or save your life."

He appreciated his uncle's words and decided to plant a seed that could possibly change his mind about taking on an extra project. "What about…"

"No more questions. Return to work." Sheikh Kamran rounded his desk, where he took a seat. "We do not want them to question why you're late returning from lunch."

When he returned to the finance hub, the staff were whispering and speculating about what had happened with one of the guests. Rashid wondered if Yolanda was the one who had gotten herself into trouble. No one paid him any attention as he made his way to his office. When he arrived, there was a note on his keyboard. Rashid scanned the area but no one stood out as odd.

He walked over to the man whose workstation was outside his office. "Did you see anyone in my office?"

"Jasper stopped by but I told him you were at lunch."

"Thanks." Rashid went to the desk and opened the note.

Stop digging unless it is your desire to be in the grave.

Chapter 9

Yolanda's nerves had finally calmed down, even though her mind kept replaying the other day's events in her head. She had a sneaking suspicion that Beverly hadn't told Angela how she had ended up in the Spice Souk where she was taken. Hell. She couldn't even explain it and it happened to her.

"Did you want me to have this meeting rescheduled?" Angela asked as they approached the final hall leading to their destination.

She took a deep breath. "I'm fine."

Yolanda had welcomed the chance to stay in the palace despite what had happened the other day. She smiled with nervous energy as she entered the foyer of Sheikh Kamran's office. One of the doors opened and Sheikh Kamran stepped through wearing a traditional middle eastern garment called a dishdasha—a white floor length tunic that touched to the edge of his sandaled feet. He motioned for her to follow him inside the office and her heart thumped as if she had sprinted through the building.

Had she done something wrong to earn this invite? Or was this about what happened at the Spice Souk? His purple aura seemed to match what she heard about him being spiritual. From the corner of her eye, a turquoise color caught her attention. She turned to meet Rashid's arrogant gaze as he stood from the leather guest chair.

"Great seeing you again." Rashid extended a hand.

Remembering his cavalier tone when he had mistaken her for the housekeeper, she couldn't control her first reaction—giving him the evil eye. Had she not been in the presence of the Sheikh, her response would have been much different. "Same."

She accepted Rashid's hand and was almost blinded by the brilliant red that lit up the room. Her body trembled as if she'd stepped on a live wire and she dropped his hand as if he'd burnt her.

"I am hoping you can work on an outreach gala with my nephew." Kamran motioned toward the empty guest chair.

"Your father tells us you're an amazing event planner," Daron said, as she settled into the seat next to Rashid.

She hadn't even noticed him leaning near the Durabian flag in the corner. Daron's blue aura brightened as he spoke. He seemed intuitive every time she was in his presence, but she wasn't sure about the spiritual aspect the blue glow indicated. Something about him screamed danger.

"It'll be a good way to keep your mind off the current situation." Daron handed her a gold folder. "These are the programs that will be highlighted on the night of the gala."

She scanned the information to bring herself up to date, as well as to avoid laying eyes on Rashid.

The prison and women's outreach programs piqued her interest. "I'd love to help out, but I'm not familiar enough with Durabia and what it has to offer to do this event justice."

"That is where Rashid comes in." Kamran took a seat behind the mahogany desk. "He will answer any questions you have on location and vendors. He will also manage the budget."

"Uncle, clearly this assignment is beyond her abilities," Rashid said, in that arrogant tone and matching posture on full display.

Yolanda saw red and not because of an aura change. The pompous prick had the nerve to insult her in front of the Sheikh.

"I'd be more than happy to help." She gave Rashid a mischievous smile, and added, "Hopefully you're as well versed in Durabian hospitality as Sheikh Kamran *seems* to think you are because it's been lacking since day one."

Daron and Kamran both lifted an eyebrow and exchanged an amused look but said nothing.

"Trust me, his confidence in my abilities is well placed," Rashid fired back, his aura surrounded by a magnificent ring of red.

"That remains to be seen."

Chapter 10

Relief filled Jasper's weather-worn face as Rashid confirmed the audit was completed.

"A courier service will pick these up." He took the pile of manila packets from Rashid's hands and placed them near the edge of the desk.

Rashid nodded. Jasper's actions confirmed that all of those unrelated requests were to keep Rashid busy and away from verifying the numbers. "I will be working in the office after hours with the latest palace guest."

"Sheikh Kamran mentioned it. You do not seem happy about this new development." Jasper rubbed his grey beard as he set the packets down and lowered himself in the executive chair. "Maybe it has to do with all those beautiful women you have vying for your attention." He waved in his assistant, Imad Habib, a slender and graceful gentleman, who entered the room, picked up the packets Jasper pointed to, pressed them against his white tunic, then swept out.

"Our meetings should not interfere with my nightlife." Rashid twisted his new watch, compliments of Daron. No one would guess it housed a flash drive, tracker, and was a scanner. "How are the wives and children?"

"They are good now." He smiled and turned to his computer, but not before he scanned Rashid's gray suit and grimaced. "Get back to work. I know you have a meeting with the Americans today."

Rashid made a beeline for his office and slid into the leather seat. Daron had suggested copying all the files to the flash drive. He would work on the project from his personal computer to decrease the culprit's chance to erase the trail. The file, which included a spreadsheet tracking the inconsistencies in the royal accounts, and a document that referenced the billing in question, would be essential. Rashid wished he could close his door, but that wasn't his normal routine. Jasper would immediately know something was amiss.

He lowered his wrist, flipped the watch face up, and removed the flash drive. People milled about outside his office door, but no one was paying much attention to his efforts. He slid the small black flash drive into the computer port, moving his water bottle into position to block anyone's view. Minutes later, all the records were copied.

From what Rashid had observed, most of the inconsistencies started shortly after Kamran ascended to the throne and continued until the present day.

━━━

Rashid watched Yolanda sashay in wearing an abaya and a hijab. He would love to see her again in the jeans that hugged her hips and shapely behind when he first encountered her. His body reacted to the memory.

"Your laptop is over there." He pointed to the silver device at the opposite end of the desk. "Concentrate on the venue. I need your top three hotels or locations by tomorrow." Inwardly, he kicked himself. His tone was more abrupt than he intended.

"Hello is an appropriate greeting." She scowled as she settled into the guest chair. "Remember, you're *not* my boss." She lifted the lid of the laptop, switched it on, and focused on the screen.

"If you had taken Sheikha Ellena's offer and had the tour of the city, maybe I would not have to take the lead." He dropped the approved vendor list next to her laptop.

"This is my third day." She snatched the papers off the desk. "Maybe I'd be taking in the culture if I hadn't been assigned to work with someone who has no clue about planning an event besides the dollars and cents."

"I do not have time to debate." Rashid logged onto his computer while wishing Yolanda's tongue wasn't so sharp.

She huffed and mumbled. "You need to get over yourself."

"I have work to do." He slid the flash drive into the port, trying not to get lost in her honey-colored eyes. "If you have questions or need anything interpreted, let me know."

"Whatever," Yolanda muttered. She grabbed a notebook out of her purse and the sticky note with the password and typed it in.

Rashid took a breath to adjust his attitude. It wasn't her fault that someone took his file. His meeting ran over and he received a note saying he was being watched. In addition to that, he had missed lunch and had to push back his dinner date two hours to accommodate this additional time with Yolanda. Or maybe the truth was he was attracted to her and didn't want to be. Yolanda slipped in her earbuds. The dynamic beat of rhythm and blues came through loud enough for him to hear. She kept her attention on the screen, apparently tuning him out. Her delicate fingers flew across the keyboard. That perfume was a distraction in itself. So floral and pretty. Unlike her demeanor.

They had been at odds every single day since they met. The next few weeks would be long if they kept going like this.

Chapter 11

The midnight heat greeted her as she stood on the balcony, taking in the beauty of the beach and sea beyond the lawn. Sleep evaded her because strange dreams disturbed her normal slumber pattern. Prior to the night she went to Brandon's house, she had a dream about being needed in Durabia. She had no idea what turn of events would land her in the palace. Yolanda definitely could have done without being manhandled, threatened, and punched by Gerald. She rubbed her right cheek remembering the pain. Now that she was in Durabia, she wasn't sure of her purpose or what the dream symbolized.

Working with Rashid was beyond exasperating. "Sheesh," she mumbled softly. Instead of treating her like a team member, he bossed her around while doing his own thing.

She wanted to take some action to erase that cocky grin. Rashid's handsome face filled her mind and heat built in her core. She hated that she was drawn to his superior acting behind. That man had enough arrogance to fill a hot air balloon.

As she looked out onto the garden, a large spot spread and darkened on the brick wall. Seconds later, a woman sauntered out of the black hole. She recognized Jackie — who was also a guest in the palace—and her pink glow that was evident from the first day they met at dinner. If it wasn't for Yolanda's ability and the strange occurrences she experienced at a young age, she may have been frightened at the woman's sudden appearance.

Yolanda flattened herself against the balcony wall to avoid detection. Jackie's black ponytail swung side to side as she scanned the area as if to ensure no one had seen her. Daron had mentioned that Jackie had run into some trouble in the states and was here until things calmed down. Now Yolanda felt like she kind of knew why. She, Angela, and Jackie were supposed to ride into Durabia's Free Zone tomorrow. Yolanda didn't know how Jackie would feel about someone else knowing about her gift.

Jackie slipped into the palace. Yolanda understood her need for secrecy. Yolanda wondered if that is how she ended up in the Spice Souk the other day. Had Jackie left a portal open?

⊏⊐

YOLANDA ACCEPTED the calendar invite for a video chat with Martina in a few days. She was excited for an opportunity to have a conversation with someone who understood, to some degree, what she was going through.

"Are you and Rashid getting along?" Angela asked as they walked to his office.

Yolanda sighed her frustration. "He's a royal pain in the behind." He was always preoccupied with something else and a stickler for not going over his allotted time so he wouldn't be late for his dates. Every so often they engaged in meaningful conversation but he usually managed to say something to ruin the moment.

She was itching to talk to Aunt Connie about why touching

Rashid had changed her aura in such a drastic way. Hopefully, it didn't mean he was the one she was here to help. She wasn't a big fan of the bossy and condescending playboy.

"Don't be so hard on him," Angela explained as she smoothed her hijab. "You caught him at a difficult time. He's got a lot more going on than usual."

Yolanda shook her head. "Those late nights are probably wearing him out, but I shouldn't be the recipient of his short fuse."

They'd been working together for the last three weeks. Every time Rashid offered to give her a tour of Durabia, she turned him down. Not that she didn't want one, but three men from the Russo syndicate had stepped up their effort to find her. She wished the Durabain police had made it to the location she had been held before they had moved. Angela had rescued her without the assistance of a team. Her primary goal was getting Yolanda out, not apprehending them. She hoped the Durabain police would find them before they found her. Yolanda had no doubt she'd die if forced to heal Zander. Even if she refused, his sons wouldn't hesitate to put a bullet in her once she had served their purpose.

Rashid met them at the door. "I will not be able to work with you tonight."

"Really?" She tipped her head back, offended by his lack of manners.

"Email me a list of the new vendors you wish for me to contact. I will set up the appointments." He glanced at his watch and the tunic caressed his muscles the way a long-lost lover would.

She took a deep breath trying to calm down and not be affected by the sex appeal oozing off him like melted caramel over an ice cream cone.

"What's come up? Another date?" Yolanda asked, feeling a tinge of envy. She didn't know why. He was handsome and all, but he was also pretentious. That alone made him far less attractive. While she could ask Angela to interpret some Arabic for her, she needed his knowledge of Durabia to ensure her ideas would be respectful of their culture.

Rashid gave her a wicked grin and leaned toward her ear. "You almost sound jealous. Do not worry, you will have my undivided attention tomorrow."

He chuckled and walked away before she could respond. With one well-placed throw, her pen was upside his head.

Chapter 12

The next night, the energy in Rashid's office sent chills down Yolanda's spine. If it weren't for the fact that she was inside the palace, she'd be scared. The men from the Russo syndicate couldn't have penetrated the high-level security system. Yet, something was off. She glanced at Angela, who was working across a small round table, to see if she sensed it too.

Jaspar knocked on the door then lifted a hand to acknowledge Yolanda and Angela's presence. "Rashid. Do not stay too late. The office deep cleaning is scheduled for this evening."

"They know we have to wrap up early." Rashid glanced in Yolanda's direction.

"Clear out in time. No excuses." Jaspar's tone made his words feel like a threat.

Yolanda grimaced and returned her focus on evaluating the various vendors. They only would be in the office for an hour tonight. Yolanda lost a sense of time as she and Angela narrowed down their list. Every once in a while, she'd glance up at Rashid behind his desk with his face intensely focused on his laptop. It should be a crime to be so damn sexy. Her gaze roamed over his sleek physique. Rashid was oddly quiet, only checking with them occasionally to find out if his help was needed. She wondered if his silence was related to the project that had captured his attention most of the night while they were planning the gala.

The lights flickered as a loud boom was heard down the hall. Rashid's head snapped up from his laptop.

Angela hopped up with her hands hovering over the holstered weapon. "I'm going to do a quick check of the area."

"It's probably the cleaning staff." Rashid glanced at his watch.

They had been working for two hours. Yolanda hadn't realized how much time had passed.

"While you pack up, I'll take a look," Angela said as the light flickered again.

"Okay." Yolanda hit save on her notes then logged out of her laptop. She gathered the various pamphlets and binders from the table then stuffed them in her bag. Only her phone and tablet remained on the table.

"My apologies that I have been so distracted." Rashid stood and stretched his limbs. "This other project I am working on is wrapping up soon and I will be able to concentrate on the gala."

His eyes widened as the lights blinked again. He headed to the door as the office went dark. "That's what I was afraid of."

Yolanda jumped at the sound of something slamming hard against the floor. "What in the hell is going on?" She frantically scrambled to find her cellphone with only the fading daylight to assist.

The backup lights kicked in. A thick sheet of glass now separated the office from the hallway.

"The power outage has triggered the emergency protocol." He glanced through the security door that had locked them in. "Key offices are immediately protected."

Yolanda walked over to the window expecting to see the lights out in the other part of the building. "Is the palace on a different power grid?"

"Yes, why?" He took long strides toward her, then peered out. Rashid whipped out his cell phone. "This is Rashid Ali Khan. I want to know when will the power be restored?" His face went taut. "Thank you."

Her mind was bombarded with questions. Who was he talking to? What did they say? Three rapid knocks interrupted her thoughts before she could open her mouth to ask a single one.

"The cleaners are not here." Angela's voice was muffled through the glass. "I'm trying to find out what's going on with the power."

Yolanda didn't miss that her eyes were trained down the hallway. She headed to the door staring out into the hallway. Jasper's office was the only other door locked down with a protective shield.

"Be safe." Rashid moved toward the threshold. Angela gave him a slight nod before heading down the corridors.

"Is something going on that I should know about?" Yolanda asked. She could feel the tension radiating off of him in waves.

He gave her a slight smile. "No, but we may be stuck here for a while. Once the power is restored, the security team has to check the vault first." He ambled over to his desk, pulled the flash drive out of his laptop, then closed the lid before sliding the drive into his pocket. "Our vault manager has left for the day, which means they have to wait until he returns to verify everything is as it should be." Rashid lowered himself into the leather executive chair.

Something was definitely going on and it had to do with Rashid's other project. Even in the dimly lit office, she could see the worry lines etched on his face.

"What would have happened if he had been here?" She sauntered over to the round table off to the side of Rashid's desk where she and Angela had been going through samples. "Or he walked out moments before the security door activated and he's locked out his office like Angela is." Yolanda didn't know if she could handle being in a room with him when he was being normal.

"Depends." He swiveled his chair in her direction. "He would be locked in the vault. If he was not, he is trained to get to one of three panic rooms strategically located throughout the office."

"Why are only Jasper's and your offices protected?"

"We have the authorization to access the vault."

Were people trying to break in to get money? Was Angela in danger? Would they try to breach Rashid's office? Yolanda pulled out her tablet to calm her thoughts. She retrieved a newspaper written in Arabic because she knew it would require her to focus.

"Are you still working on the event?"

Yolanda's head snapped up. She hadn't heard him approach and now he was standing over her looking devastatingly handsome in the low light. She needed his rude and insulting comments to help keep her attraction to him in check.

"No, I'm reading." She followed his eyes to her screen. "Angela suggested it would help to recognize Arabic words. We're working on growing my vocabulary so I can read it even if I can't speak it. It worked out well for my best friend and me when we went to Mexico."

Rashid sat across from her. "How so?" He extended his long legs brushing against hers causing her entire body to tingle as if she had been shocked.

It took her a moment to shake off the effects and respond. "I knew the words, but I couldn't say them correctly. I would spell them out for my friend or type out the sentence and she could speak it in a manner that the locals understood."

Yolanda didn't know how they ended up laughing and trading their travel adventures. The discussion shifted to cultural differences around the globe and world politics. Talking with Rashid felt like she was catching up with an old friend. Yolanda enjoyed the way his voice vibrated when he laughed, and his eyes lit up when he was excited. Their exchange was a refreshing change from their norm. She momentarily forgot the odd circumstances that held them in the office. The conversation made the hour they'd been waiting fly by.

"Would you like something to drink?" He stood sauntering over to the cabinet on the back wall. He pressed the oak door to reveal a refrigerator.

"Water please?"

"The vault, my office, Jasper's office, and the panic room all have drinks and nonperishable food stocked." He retrieved two bottles then returned to the table. "If you get hungry, let me know."

Yolanda's response was drowned out by gunfire. She ran to the door to see Angela dip into an open office. "What the hell is going on?"

Rashid was by her side in a flash. He whipped out his phone. "This is Rashid Ali Khan." He eased her away from the door. "What is happening?"

She strained to hear the other side of the conversation, but only caught bits and pieces.

The gunfire ceased. Rashid looked at her and said, "The situation has been handled."

"What happened?" Yolanda stared up at him.

"The problem was taken care of. That is all you need to know."

Rashid's authoritative tone grated on her nerves. She should have known he would say something to irritate her. "You know what..."

The words were stolen out of her mouth by the security door suddenly lifting and the room was flooded with light. Angela appeared at the threshold with a bullet hole in the arm of her shirt. Yolanda was relieved to see that it was only a flesh wound.

Chapter 13

The pattern of theft was as clear as the glass separating a balcony from a bedroom. Rashid assumed the two-week period when there were no transactions was because the discrepancies were more likely to be caught. During the span where the month-end reports were produced and reviewed, the culprits were silent. He needed to analyze a few more current transactions before handing over his findings to the Sheikh. The theory was the lockdown incidents were to acquire funds from the vaults' petty cash. Rashid hadn't figured out how. The only other people with access to the vault besides himself were Jasper, the vault manager, and Sheikh Kamran. Who had cancelled the cleaning staff? Who were the people pretending to be them? How did they get out without a trace? Had they not been in the office late, no one would have thought to check the finance section.

Imad cleared his throat and leaned into the doorjamb. "Jasper wants those EOM reports first thing in the morning."

"The end of month reports are already in his inbox." Rashid double checked his email to confirm he had hit send. Jasper was still monitoring his actions, which is why he made sure all requests were submitted before the given deadline.

"He must have forgotten to forward it to me." Imad eyed him with suspicion before walking away.

Rashid, who had great respect for Yolanda due to her creativity, intellect, and budgeting savvy, was excited to have some time to focus on helping Yolanda with the gala and change her impression of him. Every time he was in her presence he wanted to know more about her. He wanted to lose himself in her eyes. He also wanted to learn a little more about her and any future plans. Was she planning to make Durabia her new home? He tried to discreetly find out more about her from some of the staff, but she tended to stay to herself and Angela as well as Beverly were tight-lipped with information.

His parents had given him a few years to establish himself in the kingdom and find love on his own. If he was not successful in the last one, his parents would arrange a marriage. With all the uproar about a woman who was not a national being on the throne, this was not the best time for him to be attracted to Yolanda. Why was marriage and her name showing up in the same sentence? He could not deny his desire was to explore her mind and soul to discover everything she loved so he could please her. He stared at the computer screen wondering if his parents would accept Yolanda. They were a mix of conventional and untraditional. He never knew where they would land on a subject.

Rashid glanced up as Yolanda entered the office. Angela and Beverly settled outside the door. He was mesmerized by the sway of Yolanda's hips. She sat in her usual spot and logged into the computer.

"No hello or good evening?" He inhaled the passion fruit scent that wafted in with her.

Yolanda smirked, pulling out a binder from her bag. "Those words didn't seem to be in your vocabulary."

"Who is being rude this evening?" Rashid chuckled, retrieving a document from the printer. "I contacted the venues. Two have the date available." He handed her the venue sheet.

She gave him a leery glare then studied the paper. "Jumillah Hotel is situated on an island, right?"

"Yes." Rashid loved the ballroom at that location but with their guest list, it could be a security nightmare. His gaze drifted to Yolanda's luscious lips wanting to feel them against his.

"I prefer the other location. Plus, I like the choices on their banquet menu better." She pulled the Jumillah's brochure from the binder and slipped it into her bag.

"I agree. I will reserve the room and date." Rashid dialed the hotel and requested a contract for the Emperor's ballroom and a specific date with the catering manager. "What is next on the checklist?"

"Umm, don't you have something else to work on?" She frowned and retrieved a notebook and pen from her bag.

He grabbed two cans of lemonade from a small refrigerator at the back of the office. "Today my full focus is on the gala." Rashid smiled and placed one in front of her.

"Are you feeling okay?" She frowned, opened the can, then took a sip.

He nodded and reclaimed his seat as she checked something off her notebook. "What is next?"

"The invitation." She flipped open the binder to the samples.

Rashid came and sat down in the chair beside her. His eyes kept drifting to her beautiful face as they selected paper and font styles. He resisted the urge to touch her as they discussed food, decorations, and other event details for the next hour. The way her eyes lit up as she spoke about the plans for the gala warmed his heart.

Yolanda was a mystery that he was thrilled to dive in and explore. What trouble had caused her to go into hiding? Did she witness something terrible? Was she getting away from an abusive boyfriend? "Can I ask you a personal question?"

She eyed him carefully. "Sure, since you were actually helpful tonight."

"Will your boyfriend visit you while you are here?"

"No." Yolanda's focus never strayed from the computer screen.

Rashid sighed. He should have known she wouldn't make it simple to get the answer he wanted. He stood picking up the empty cans and dumping them into the garbage can. "Why not?"

"I answered your one question." Yolanda chuckled. "It's my turn to ask one."

"Okay."

She closed the lid of the laptop, crossed her legs, and tilted her head toward him. "Why are you working as a financial analyst?" Her eyes shifted to the framed degree on the wall before returning to him.

"I was willing to work wherever the Sheikh placed me." His uncle was kind enough to offer Rashid a job when he returned home after his mother unexpectedly fell ill.

"Interesting." Yolanda closed the binder. "I feel there's more to the story."

"Indeed." He felt those honey-colored eyes searing into his soul. He didn't want to get into his mother's recovery or his complicated family history. Rashid had to show the Sheikh that he did not share his older brother's work ethic and that he was nothing like his power-hungry uncles, who had plotted and planned his downfall. Bilal was good at giving orders but not executing the assignments given to him. "Now back to my second question." He leaned on the desk next to her.

"I'm not in a relationship." Yolanda gave him a mischievous grin. "I'm trying to be like you, out with someone new every night."

Rashid was determined to prove how wrong she was about him as soon as he turned over the flash drive with the incriminating information. The last thing he wanted was to put Yolanda's life in danger, especially after the incident with someone shooting at Angela as they were trying to break into the vault.

Chapter 14

Rashid made his way to his suite in the palace, pondering Yolanda's statements. Most believed he was a ladies' man, but he had developed many friendships during his summers in London and while attending Yale in America. Some of his friends now lived in Durabia, and others flew in often for a visit. Tonight, he had a real date with a woman who was gorgeous and intelligent, but his distraction ruined the evening and ended his date early. If only he could blame it on his search for those responsible for secretly moving millions out of the royal accounts. However, it was Yolanda's quiet but sassy ways and those full luscious lips, demanding to be kissed, that stayed on his mind. Durabia had no shortage of beautiful women but something about Yolanda spoke to his soul.

Nicco, one of Daron's security personnel, was posted in the hall. He nodded as Rashid pulled out the key. He entered his room, which was shrouded in darkness. The laptop was open, and someone clad in all black stared at the screen. The computer's light showed that the man's eyes grew to the size of saucers as he stared at Rashid.

"Stop," Rashid yelled, sprinting across the room.

The man dashed for the open balcony doors. Rashid snatched the prowler by the arm as he reached the rail. The intruder slammed his elbow into Rashid's face, but he refused to let go. They tussled, then crashed into a chair. Rashid lost his grip when he grabbed hold of the chair to keep his balance.

The man braced on the wall to keep from hitting the floor. He bolted for the banister and hopped over before Rashid came to his feet.

Nicco flew past Rashid and followed the man down the black rope attached to the banister moments later. The intruder raced across the lawn with Nicco hot on his heels.

Rashid rushed back into the room to the laptop, which had previously been locked in his desk drawer. When he flicked the lights on, he noticed a grey flash drive on the red and gold carpet under his desk. He placed it next to his computer. On the screen, three asterisks were in the login area. Rashid had interrupted the trespasser's attempt to log in. So he hadn't made off with any information.

Angela ran inside with her weapon drawn. She scanned the room, then asked, "Is everything okay?"

"Someone may be verifying that I have stopped my inquiry." He flipped the lid of the laptop down.

She put away the Beretta, rested an index finger against her lips, then pulled out a wand from her inner jacket pocket. The moment she waved it over his desk, the device beeped loud enough to wake those sleeping. Angela moved it away and sound quieted, then she pulled out a cell phone. "We have a Class B situation."

She reclaimed the wand, then motioned for Rashid to follow her out to the balcony. "Your presence is requested."

Rashid watched as she moved the wand over the chairs and table. She listened intently to whomever she was speaking to, then slid the wand back into her jacket.

As soon as she completed her phone call, Rashid asked, "Do you know if he got away?"

She shook her head. "Nicco is currently escorting him to an interrogation room. Did he take anything?"

"I do not think so, but I found a flash drive on the floor near my desk." Rashid's gaze shifted back into the room.

"We'll sweep the room to make sure that he didn't leave any more *gifts*." Angela waved in two men who knocked on the open suite door. "When we're inside, don't talk about your investigation."

Rashid took a seat on a white chaise while the security team went through all areas — bedroom, bathroom, and living room. Angela slipped on a pair of gloves, removed the rope from the banister, and put it in a plastic bag.

Reviewing his recent conversations, Rashid wondered if he'd said anything to give himself away. He had reached out to a company earlier that day questioning the amount received on a recent payment. Rashid hadn't thought anything about following up on current billing. Now he grimaced, realizing his error.

"Rashid," Angela called out while standing over a dark-haired man who sat at his desk.

He went over to them and stared at the man's laptop. "Yes, Angela."

"It looks like they were trying to place a virus on your laptop to wipe out the data," Angela explained.

Rashid glanced at his watch, which held a flash drive with all his research backup.

According to Angela, it had to be an inside job. The trespasser entered through the balcony during a commotion that drew the guards away. No one had broken through the security perimeter, which mean someone had to allowed the intruder onto the grounds earlier. He had a good idea of who.

"I know you didn't want to install sensors on the balcony, but after this, we'll have to. You need to be alerted if you have any more visitors," she said, as the second man closed and secured the balcony door.

From this moment until he confirmed who was behind the

missing money, he'd have to make sure his suite was secure. He'd always felt safe on the palace grounds, so he'd never been conscious of the precautions he took for granted. He also thought his balcony was too high up for his room to be invaded, but he would not make that mistake again.

"Thank you. Is Daron still in Durabia?"

The man packed up his laptop before joining the other gentleman at the door.

"He returns from Nadaum tomorrow." She proceeded to the exit then paused in the doorway. "Remember, someone is in the hallway if you need help."

Rashid nodded and then locked up behind her. This incident solidified his next move. Time to hand over the data so Kamran and Daron could take the culprits down. He moved the information from his laptop to a flash drive for Kamran and planned to give Daron the backup. Both would remain on him at all times until he could safely deliver them into their hands.

Chapter 15

Yolanda couldn't believe one of the royal guards was in critical condition. From what she overheard, someone's car smashed him into the front gate. Her laptop beeped as Martina appeared on the screen. She was attractive with blue eyes and long dark hair. Yolanda was caught off guard by the burst of murky gray in Martina's green aura. It made her pause and wonder about her past and if she could truly be transparent with her.

Dad wouldn't have suggested I talk to her if she was a danger to me.

"Are you okay?" Martina asked, with concern laced in her voice.

"Yeah. There was an incident last night." Yolanda gave her an apologetic smile. "It has thrown me off."

"We can reschedule," Martina said as she glanced at her cell.

"No. I know you're a busy woman." Yolanda focused on the conversation.

For the next thirty-minute, they had a refreshing chat, exchanging stories about their experiences. Yolanda ended the call feeling grateful to have a conversation where she didn't have to avoid discussing her gift. However, it left her with so many questions about Martina. Why would a healer have murky gray bursting in her aura? A light knock drew her attention.

"Come in." Yolanda put the laptop into her tote bag.

Nicco entered. "Are you ready?"

"Yes." Yolanda grabbed her tote and moved closer to the door. She could hear voices in the hallway.

"Last night's incident at the checkpoint was a distraction to draw the guards away from the security monitors to allow the intruder to break into Rashid's room. That was the only information the intruder was willing to give up." The guards stopped talking to Nicco when she fully stepped outside her room. She greeted them with a smile and headed to the end of the hallway.

As they made the trek to Rashid's office, she wondered if she was meant to heal the guard. While she thought it would be someone like the Sheikh or Sheikha who needed her help, the reality was, it could be someone she least expected. Sometimes, the smaller pieces had a greater effect on the bigger picture than people expected. Once healed, the guard could thwart an attack on the royal family in the future or maybe provide key intel that could help the kingdom. Balancing who would receive her help had always been a precarious thing. Sometimes people were supposed to die. In the beginning, she quietly tried to heal everyone. But soon realized when a person's time came, she was not supposed to interfere with their path. Her cousin was one of those people and it hurt her entire soul when he finally said, "Yo-Yo, grandma's waiting for me."

She glanced at Angela, who wore jeans, a floral t-shirt, and a hijab, and asked, "What happened to Rashid last night?"

The commotion ahead distracted them. The Arabic spewing from several men became louder as they neared the office.

Gripping her arm, Angela shifted Yolanda back so she was in a protected position. "I'm going to need you to stay behind me."

Over her shoulder, Yolanda watched Rashid rush toward a pair of belligerent men as the royal guards ran from the other direction. "What's going on?"

Beverly and Jackie rushed toward them as two men fought in the foyer of the finance offices.

Jackie pursed her small lips. "The devil is at play."

Yolanda noted the concern in Jackie's almond-shaped eyes then turned her attention to the commotion. While everyone was heading toward the altercation, she found it odd that Jasper, along with Imad, slid back into the office as though they had more important things to handle.

The royal guards separated the two men and hauled them away as Rashid marched to where the women stood.

"Ladies." Rashid smiled, and his gaze seared into Yolanda's soul. "Are you ready to see the venue?" Somehow, he acted as though nothing out of the ordinary had transpired.

"Yes. Jackie will be riding with us." Yolanda motioned to the dark-haired beauty. "She's meeting a friend there for lunch."

"The guards are waiting near the limo." Rashid turned and led them out of the building.

"We'll meet you there," Yolanda said. "I want to stop by the hospital and visit the injured guard before we come back."

"Why?" Rashid glanced over his shoulder.

"Why not? Is there a crime against it?" Yolanda hoped he wouldn't push the issue.

Rashid frowned and opened his mouth, then snapped it shut as if he reconsidered whatever he was about to say. After a few moments, he said, "That is not a problem. We can do it *after* our appointment."

Yolanda smirked, a little leery of Rashid being nice for a change. Although the guards had dealt with the situation in the palace, she couldn't help thinking that danger lurked right around the corner.

———

THE UNCONSCIOUS GUARD stretched out in a hospital bed in Durabian Medical turned Yolanda's aura to green but it had what looked like small rocks floating around. Now she had to figure out a way to get rid of Rashid in order to work on the man, whose name she found out was Malik. Angela and Rashid's bodyguards waited outside the room. The only sounds were his shallow breathing and the beeping of the machines that monitored his progress.

Rashid's phone vibrated and he glanced at the screen. "I need to take this." He stepped out of the room with the phone pressed to his ear and began a conversation in Arabic.

Angela followed him, with her cellular in hand, as if she also needed to make a call. Yolanda used the opportunity to tip closer to the bed and placed an incision then stitched up the tear that had blood pooling in Malik's stomach. Something the doctors evidently didn't know about yet. She leaned to his ear and whispered, "You're going to be all right."

She speculated whether he was the reason she was in Durabia. Would her life go back to normal within the next few weeks? Or was there more to come?

Daron's contacts had spotted Gerald, Adam, and their cousin in several tourist areas. By the time a team was dispatched, they were gone. Evidently, the organization had far-reaching connections for them to be in the Middle East. For that reason, Yolanda steered clear of tourist attractions. She was ready to get back to her old life. However, until she fulfilled her purpose here, she'd be tethered to this place.

Leaving the room, she felt the same sense of relief and balance that came whenever she healed someone. Except for Brandon. She'd crossed a line with that one and was still paying the price for that error in judgment.

She glanced to see Angela and Rashid at the end of the hall. As she stepped into the hall, Adam appeared in the hallway in between her and them. Yolanda pivoted and walked swiftly in the other direction. Adam advanced on her like a man on a mission.

Go into the staircase.

Yolanda's eyes scanned until she found the sign for the stairs. She pushed through the door and stepped onto the landing.

Go up.

She took the stairs two at a time. Adam grabbed her leg and snatched it from under her. She fell forward and caught herself before she crashed into the stairs. He tried to yank her toward him, but she kicked him off.

"You can end this by helping us out." Adam caught up with her on the next landing and slammed her against the wall.

Yolanda kneed him in the groin. His body folded forward as his hand went to block another kick. She slammed both hands down on his back as she brought her knee to his face. He grunted in pain as she sprinted out the door.

She ran past a nurse, almost crashing into the carts she was pushing.

"Please walk miss."

"Sorry." Yolanda slowed to a fast walk as she passed the nurses' station to the other staircase.

Yolanda did as the voice instructed and entered the stairwell just as Adam flew past the nurses' station. She raced down the stairs aiming for Angela and Rashid. Yolanda had to make it to them.

Chapter 16

When Yolanda burst out of the stairwell, Angela was heading back towards the room. Rashid ended his call and he smiled. Her heart thumped in response and she barely heard the one word he spoke while he put away his phone.

"Ready?" he asked as Angela pivoted back in their direction.

"Yes," she said as Angela frowned at her as if to ask where had she been. She mouthed to her, Adam is here. "The guard was looking better when I left."

Angela nodded, moving to her side.

Rashid's driver stood from one of the seats in the waiting area. "I'll bring the car around." He bypassed the elevator and headed for the stairs.

Her eyes stayed on the stairwell as Angela pressed the call button. Adam came bolting out onto the floor then paused when he saw her. He gave a wicked smile and pulled out his cell as the elevator doors opened.

Angela shifted Yolanda into the elevator.

Yolanda took a calming breath and glanced at Rashid, trying to think of a conversation that would distract her from what had just happened. "The meeting at the hotel went well."

"Yes." Rashid and the guard stood against the elevator walls and Angela typed into her phone. "The event is coming together nicely."

"A few more details to lock in place and we're done." Yolanda studied the lines of his handsome face. Rashid had been charming and charismatic while confirming the final plans for the gala. Not once did he use his aristocratic tone. Seemed he only saved that for her. She only was allowed a glimpse at the nicer version of him on occasion.

Several minutes later the silver doors opened, and Angela took the lead, heading through the building's exit. Rashid allowed Yolanda to go through first. Yolanda's lip curled into a smile at the unexpected courtesy. Beverly nodded at Yolanda as she and another guard trailed entered the hospital. Yolanda hoped they would find Adam and his cousin.

Rashid fell in step with her and asked, "Would you join me for lunch?"

"Where is the real Rashid?" Yolanda teased.

Stay alert.

Yolanda scanned the area around her looking for Adam. Her mouth dropped open at the sight of a familiar face heading toward the hospital door.

Gerald.

Fear shot through her despite being surrounded by guards.

Angela must have sensed something was wrong. Her stride slowed and she shifted closer to Yolanda then looked in Gerald's direction. "Move faster."

Before Yolanda could, the Busch brothers' cousin appeared and charged them. He reached for Yolanda, but Angela grabbed his arm. He slid out of her grip and tackled the guard, who was rushing Yolanda and Rashid to the car. Angela shoved Gerald against the vehicle seconds before he reached them.

Rashid pushed Yolanda through the open limo door at the exact moment something swished past her ear. A thud resounded as it hit the metal.

He fell into the limo as she scooted out the way.

"You okay?" she asked.

He nodded and slammed the door closed.

Angela waved them off and sat on top of Gerald, who was spread-eagled on the ground.

"Go," Rashid shouted.

Yolanda's hands trembled as Angela lifted Gerald from the ground. She felt Rashid watching her and in the next second, he turned her away from the back window and wrapped his arm around her.

"You're safe now." He gently stroked her arm.

She hadn't thought that visiting the guard would put her in danger. Although she was happy that she had healed him, she couldn't help but wonder how on earth Gerald knew where to find her? *Hopefully, now I can stop looking over my shoulder.*

The ride back to the palace was silent and uneventful, except for the fact that Rashid did not relinquish his hold on her. She felt a certain amount of comfort being near him.

Nicco greeted them at the limo as the other guards formed a perimeter shield around Yolanda and Rashid. He informed them that Angela was waiting for the Durabian police to process Gerald and Adam. Their cousin had managed to get away.

Rashid reached for her hand as she headed to her suite. His dark gaze searched hers. "Do you really want to be alone right now?"

Her eyes went to Nicco, who stepped back giving them space, as she said, "Not really."

He led her to a secluded area of the back lawn through a row of trees. They sat on a bench with a small table in front of it that faced the beach and the sea. Nicco stood at the entrance to the path.

"I did not realize event planners were so high in demand that people would cross the ocean to drag them back," Rashid teased, handing her a lemonade from the small refrigerator underneath the table. "You must have sprinkled gold dust on them."

Yolanda gave a half-smile at his attempt to lighten the mood.

Rashid covered her hand with his. "In some ways, I understand the spell you cast over them."

The energy shifted as Rashid gazed deep into her eyes, sending a ripple of need through her body.

Not ready to address the change, she asked, "What was it like growing up inside the palace?"

He searched her gaze for a moment. His words were slow in coming, then he told her about his upbringing as part of the royal family and the things that had transpired when Ellena came to Durabia and how her and Kamran's union changed their world. They talked until the daylight dimmed. She was surprised at Rashid's ability to keep her calm. Every time her mind drifted to her attackers he would tell a childhood tale that put her at ease.

"I appreciate you keeping me company while Angela deals with my situation."

"It is not a problem," he said. "You needed someone, and I happened to be here. I am sure you would do the same if the situation were reversed."

She was surprised to admit he was right. A few weeks ago, it would have been questionable.

Rashid helped her stand and they strolled back into the palace with Nicco following at a discreet distance. Her phone rang as they reached the door of her suite. On seeing Angela's name, she answered.

While Yolanda listened carefully to Angela's update, Rashid scanned her face.

After she hung up, he asked, "Is everything all right?"

She nodded and let out a breath. "Zander, the man who was hunting me, died in the hospital today. His sons have been taken into custody."

According to Gerald, outside the three of them, the only person from the syndicate who knew about her gift was their cousin. If he was telling the truth, it meant once their cousin was apprehended, she could return home.

Why does that thought fill me with such sadness?

Chapter 17

Rashid hated that his meeting with Sheikh Kamran had been delayed. The culprits were within his sights which was why he'd called Daron, requesting that he be present at the finance luncheon. He touched the royal pin on his tunic and the flash drive tucked in the bulletproof vest underneath. He had no idea what extremes they'd go to make sure the information never made it to its intended recipient.

As he stared out the window of the limo, the moment he'd shared with Yolanda after those men had come after her entered into his mind. It had been induced by danger, but something had been simmering between them since the day they met. Almost a sign that he was in danger of losing his heart to her. Rashid looked forward to taking down the people responsible for stealing from the royal family so that he could move on to explore the chemistry with Yolanda that churned beneath the surface whenever they shared the same space.

"We are here," the driver said, pulling up to one of Durabia's tallest buildings.

Seconds later, the door of the Limo opened. When Rashid stepped out, two royal guards flanked him on both sides.

"Gentlemen, let me know the moment Mr. Kincaid arrives." Rashid glanced at his watch.

In addition to the billing discrepancies, he discovered large amounts of money being moved digitally in the last year to fund a committee that didn't exist. Based on the paper and digital trail, he had a list of suspects. The transfers had been going on too long not to have deeper roots than he could find, without asking questions that would leave no doubt he was preparing to take them down.

One of the guards held the glass door open. Rashid passed through the elegant lobby decorated in black with pops of red and cream, to the reception area. Jasper was speaking to someone Rashid could not identify because his back was to him. By the frown lines on Jasper's face and his steely gaze, the conversation wasn't a pleasant one.

"Stay close until I reach my table," Rashid instructed the guards. Normally, they gave him some space to work the room while always being nearby. They needed to be by his side until they had no choice but to watch him from a distance. The Sheikh having an emergency during the time they were scheduled to meet wasn't a coincidence. Rashid hadn't put it in his calendar, but Jasper mentioned the appointment to him during a project updating session.

The waitstaff passed with an array of drinks on a tray. Rashid declined, thinking about how Kamran's brothers and their wives attempted to poison Ellena at one time. Avoiding lunch would be problematic but through sleight of hand and a properly placed napkin, most people wouldn't know he wasn't eating.

Rashid's cell phone vibrated, and he glanced at the screen. Daron texted to say he was in route. Imad approached and greeted him with a firm handshake. The gold basket weave ring Imad wore scratched Rashid's hand as he released his grip.

"The speaker is excellent." Imad smiled and stepped back. "You should enjoy his speech."

Rashid glanced at his hand to make sure that the scratch hadn't broken the skin. No blood. "I always appreciate every one of the speakers."

"Take good care of him." Imad patted both bodyguards' arms with his other hand.

He frowned because Imad had never made a statement like that before. Maybe it wasn't so odd, since Yolanda had been attacked in front of the hospital.

Jasper approached him with his brown eyes darting around the room. "I would like you to meet David." He motioned to the shorter man to his right.

"It is a pleasure to make your acquaintance." Rashid shook David's hand.

"David is the former president of ..."

Rashid heard nothing else. His body felt as though it was being roasted over an open flame. He scanned the crowd for the waitstaff. He waved the nearest one over, took a bottled water and a few napkins. Rashid checked the seal before twisting the top off and taking a sip.

"Are you okay?" one of the guards asked, gaze narrowed.

Rashid wiped the sweat from his brow with one of the napkins. "Excuse me, gentlemen."

He aimed for the restroom, suddenly feeling light-headed. Glancing over his shoulder, he ensured his guards were with him, along with Jasper and David. His legs weakened under him and he caught himself on the wall. The guards held him up, one on each side.

"I need to sit down." Rashid detoured to a seating area off a hallway. Both guards blinked as if they were fighting to stay awake. He pressed the button on his watch to let Daron's team know his location and that something was wrong.

"I will grab you more water," Jasper said, heading toward the bar with David on his heels.

Imad rushed over with two huge men trailing him. "Is everything all right?"

"Yes," he lied. Rashid gave him a weak smile, hoping they would go away. "I just need a private moment."

"I have a room where that would be possible," Imad offered.

Rashid hesitated but figured this was the only way to know for sure whether the man meant him harm. Daron was already on the way and that was more than enough insurance.

They followed Imad until he stopped at a door halfway down the hallway, used a key to open the digital lock, and held the door open for the guards to bring Rashid inside.

The room contained a couple of tables and boxes scattered throughout the space.

Rashid's vision went hazy as the guards lowered him into a chair. The men with Imad stepped in behind them.

His own guards swayed and fell over.

Imad's men caught them before they hit the floor, laying them carefully on the gold and black carpet near Rashid's feet.

Attempting to check on them, Rashid lunged forward but Imad pressed him back into the chair by the shoulder. "They are fine but by the time they wake up you will be dead."

Imad gave him a wicked smile that chilled his blood.

Rashid clicked the royal pin on his tunic to activate the implanted listening device. Imad would go down whether he made it out alive or not. "Imad, they already know you are involved in stealing millions."

"You have been poisoned." He crouched in front of Rashid, wearing an evil sneer. "What you know will die with you."

"Daron and his team are on their way," Rashid managed to say as the weakness in his limbs spread to his torso. Breathing had become so difficult. His hand shook as he pressed the emblem on the watch.

"We both know you suspected Jasper was behind everything. He was given an incentive to keep you out of our business." Imad motioned with his head for his men to go to the door. "Even if someone makes it to you within the next ten minutes, you will not make it to the hospital in time to be saved."

Imad left the room. The lock clicked in his wake.

If I can get to the hallway, someone will find me and call for help.

Rashid stood, but swayed on his feet and crashed into the chair.

Lowering his head, he spoke directly into the listening device. "I'm locked in a room in the middle of the hall that is right before the restrooms."

Rashid hoped to cut the search time down, especially since he did not know how precise Daron's tracker was in pinpointing a location. The boxes blurred as he trembled uncontrollably. He prayed for a miracle. He needed one to survive.

Chapter 18

Yolanda, Jackie, Beverly and Angela went to the Gold and Spice Souk before ending up at the Durabain Mall. She felt exposed as if she was streaking through the town square in her jeans and t-shirt without the hijab which wasn't required in Durabia's free zone. Although Gerald and Adam were in custody, being among tourists still made her uncomfortable.

He's in danger. Rashid needs you now.

She frowned and looked at Beverly, wishing she would give more details about what kind of danger he was in.

Angela's phone rang, and she listened for a moment before saying, "I'm close, but Yolanda and Jackie are with me. We're headed that way."

"What's wrong?" Yolanda asked as Angela dropped the shirt she'd contemplated buying onto the table and pulled out the car keys even though she already knew the answer.

"We have to leave. Rashid is in trouble." She led them out of the store, walking at a brisk pace. "Daron is stuck in traffic. He needs someone to get to Rashid right away."

"Where is he?" Yolanda trotted to keep up with Angela's long and fast strides.

Angela maneuvered around a group of American tourists and spoke over her shoulder. "At a hotel about five minutes away."

"What happened?" Jackie speed-walked alongside Yolanda.

Angela hesitated before saying, "He was given some type of fast-acting poison."

Looping her arm through Jackie's, Yolanda pulled her closer and whispered, "Can you teleport people?"

We'll get there in time.

Yolanda glanced at Beverly, who was pulling up the rear. She nodded and Yolanda put her focus back on Jackie.

The woman's eyes widened. Her mouth gaped open but realizing that this was no time for denials, she said, "I've only teleported myself and a few items."

"Get me to Rashid," Yolanda demanded in a low tone.

Jackie shook her head and whispered, "I've destroyed many objects while trying to understand my gift. I could kill you or deliver you to the wrong location."

"I'm willing to take the risk. And we don't have time to argue."

"Fine." Jackie touched Angela's shoulder. "I need a discreet area with no cameras."

"Ladies, we don't have time for delays," Angela warned without breaking her stride.

"Even being this close to him, we may not make it in time if we drive." Yolanda grasped Angela's arm and pleaded, "Trust me."

Beverly whispered something into Angela's ear.

"Fine. Let's go into a changing room." Angela pointed to a women's clothing store.

Yolanda and Jackie followed Angela into the handicapped dressing room, which was larger than normal, giving them ample space. Beverly scanned the area before stepping in behind them

Jackie gave Yolanda a leery glance. "Where is Rashid?"

Angela passed the phone to Jackie, who glanced at the location then handed it back.

"We'll go together. Hopefully, you'll make it through alive." Jackie stepped closer to Yolanda. "Let's do this."

With eyes closed and a vein throbbing on her neck, Jackie created a portal in front of the mirror, which shimmered then opened in an ever-widening circle. Angela's eyes widened to the size of dinner plates, but Beverly had no reaction.

Yolanda said a prayer for safe travels as they stepped into the portal. She experienced a moment of extreme darkness before the light appeared when they entered the room where Rashid was slumped in the chair. His aura was murky, but she wouldn't know if she could save him until she got closer. Yolanda raced to him, hopping over the fallen guards in the process as Beverly exited the portal.

"Is he okay?"

Both Jackie and Yolanda's heads swiveled toward Angela, who slid in through the closing portal.

Yolanda hadn't expected Angela to come, given the doubt she'd expressed earlier about their mode of arrival.

"No." Yolanda and Rashid's aura turned green despite the poison attacking his body. "I need you to help me lay him flat on the ground."

Yolanda wasn't sure what to do. The poison was infecting too many vital areas. She decided to draw the poison out near the kidneys. Even if his heart shut down, she had a better chance of jump-starting it than getting the kidneys to work after they stopped.

"Help me roll him onto his stomach." She lifted his tunic and focused all her attention on making an incision near the kidneys. Concentrating all her energy, Yolanda drew the toxin out of his body. Sweat poured from her forehead as she willed him to live.

Angela laid two fingers on his neck. "His pulse is fading. Jackie. Beverly. Check the guards."

Jackie kneeled, touched one guard's wrist and whispered something to Beverly.

Beverly checked the other. "Their pulses are strong."

Yolanda could have told them the two men were fine. They hadn't been given whatever was assaulting Rashid's body.

"Jackie. Go to the front desk and notify them you found three men passed out in a room." Angela rolled Jackie's man on his side while she gave the order.

Beverly had shifted the other guard into that position.

"I'll go meet Daron and bring him back here." Beverly slipped out of the room behind Jackie.

Rashid's olive skin was pasty, which caused a sliver of alarm to shoot down her spine. This was the most challenging part of healing. Their auras faded into a lighter and lighter shade of green. She'd never had anyone's aura shift from green to this murky color. Her experience with Brandon came to mind and the ordeal reminded her of the danger she now faced. Rashid was dying on her. Saving him could mean killing herself. In that instance, she knew without any inkling of doubt, this was the reason she was meant to come to Durabia.

The toxin drained out of his body as the feeling of fatigue increased in Yolanda's muscles. The incision near his kidney immediately healed, but his heart was barely beating. She tried turning him onto his back, but her feeble strength wouldn't allow it.

"I've got him." Angela placed Rashid on his back. "Are you okay? You're very pale."

"I'm fine." Yolanda shifted toward his chest. Her body ached like she'd worked out too hard. Before she could fully get into position, Rashid's heart had stopped. She placed her hand over his chest, especially now that she was willing to accept her aura turned red in his presence might mean they're a love match. "Don't you die on me," she whispered.

She sent an energetic jolt through his body. Now that she'd

found him, she wanted to see if she and Rashid could have a love like her aunt and uncle. "Come on."

She brushed the perspiration away from her face and prepared to try again. If the next jolt didn't start his heart, in her state she wouldn't be able to save him. Taking a deep breath, she shocked the heart again.

Darkness engulfed her and she collapsed on Rashid's chest.

Chapter 19

Most of the people connected to the palace thought Rashid was dead. And with the final plans underway, he would not correct them on that score. He tried to focus on what Dro, the King of Hyde Park, was saying but his mind was on the day Yolanda saved him. He couldn't forget the image of her body on the gurney being rolled out of the hotel and how much his heart hurt at the sight. Healing him almost cost Yolanda her life. She was in a coma for a full week. It had scared him more than his near death experience. He didn't want to think about what would have happened if her Aunt Connie hadn't arrived to heal her.

"Did you hear me?" Dro turned his gaze on Rashid.

In the hotel suite, he sat on a couch behind Dro, Daron, Beverly and Angela, who were stationed in front of surveillance monitors. "I am sorry I missed that."

Daron gave Rashid a steely glare. "If you're not up to confronting Imad, let us know now."

"I am. Not only did he steal from the palace coffers, but he tried to rob me of my life and Yolanda's as well." Rashid wanted to see Imad's face when he realized his plan had not worked. Dro and

Daron used the information he found to track down three additional people involved.

"This is a huge hit to their plans against Sheikh Kamran." Dro stood and stretched before walking a lap around the room.

Rashid was angry for not realizing that Imad had poisoned him. When the ring scratched him, he should have known something was amiss. Especially after he made a point of touching both guards with the opposite hand.

His mind flashed back to the moment his eyes opened as Yolanda fell onto his chest.

"Yolanda," he croaked, his voice dry and irritated.

Angela rolled Yolanda off his chest and checked her pulse.

"How is she?" Rashid propped himself on his elbow, not knowing what happened. He feared she was dead.

"I think she drained all resources to save you, but she's alive." Angela helped him sit up. "We need to get her help so she can stay that way."

Imad's voice speaking in Arabic brought Rashid's attention back to the present. Angela translated for Dro and Daron.

"With Rashid gone, Sheikh Kamran and his troublemaking wife's reign will come to an end." Imad paced in front of three men.

Rashid recognized David and the two others who had been with Imad the day he was poisoned. "Remember, we are *cautiously* scouting for new members to finance this movement."

Imad and the men continued to discuss their plans to approach those with deep pockets. He repeatedly referred to the resources being essential to making Sheikh and Sheikha pay for the unacceptable changes they made to Durabia. Imad handed each man what looked like credit card machines then exited the suite.

"We have enough to bring them in," Dro said.

"Get everyone in position," Daron said into his cell phone then turned to Rashid. "Ready to make your appearance?"

"Yes." Rashid followed the men out of the suite to the elevator and the corridor that led to the Outreach Gala.

He entered the ballroom decorated in red and cream to shocked whispers.

Imad's eyes widened as Rashid stalked toward him. The man scouted for an escape route, then bolted through the crowd to the hallway exit. He snatched Jackie closer, pulled a knife out of his pocket, and held it to her throat in one swift move. Backing up until he was outside, he pushed Jackie down to the ground.

Rashid dashed after him and tackled him to the pavement in between the vehicles, where he squirmed and demanded to be released.

Beverly helped Jackie up. Jackie brushed the gravel from her knees as Beverly assisted her back into the building.

"Surprised to see me?" Rashid asked while securing Imad's arms behind his back.

"This won't stop us." A sinister laugh seeped from Imad's lips.

An entourage spilled from the building. Sheikh Kamran and a cluster of guards stood in front of the group.

"Then you will accept punishment for every unknown attack against me until everyone involved is captured," Sheikh Kamran said as Rashid moved aside to allow the Durabian police to secure Imad.

Fear flickered in Imad's eyes as the other men involved were escorted out to police vehicles.

"Whatever evil plan you had will no longer be financed by the royal coffers." Rashid smirked and returned to the building. When he reentered the ballroom, Yolanda, wearing a gold dress with fuchsia accents, immediately caught his eye. She kneeled next to Jackie, wiping her knee with a napkin. Rashid knew she was probably healing her minor scrapes. After saving him, Yolanda had opened up to him about her gift and the reason those men were trying to hunt her down. He was not surprised when she made sure

Daron helped get Nicole into witness protection since the Busch brothers' cousin was still roaming free.

When Yolanda saw him, she smiled and lit up the room. His heart lifted as he made his way to her. Rashid was glad she had survived and recovered quickly enough for them to experience the Outreach Gala together.

She said something to Jackie, picked up a glass. then walked towards him.

"Sorry I am late for our date." He couldn't bear to miss a moment with her, especially since his time with her was limited. Rashid hated the fact that she planned to leave Durabia in two weeks. He was grateful Yolanda had decided to wait until Angela was scheduled to return to America to visit her family instead of leaving immediately. It still did not feel like enough time.

"You had important business to handle." She took the last sip of cherry-colored mocktail and lowered her glass to a nearby table.

"Agreed. The event is spectacular. We make a good team." Rashid took her hand and led her to the balcony off the ballroom.

Rashid had no doubts about wanting to spend his second chance at life getting to know her, learning her secrets, and exploring their chemistry. And he'd do whatever it took to accomplish that goal.

Warmth spread through his body when Yolanda murmured, "And maybe I've changed my mind about wanting to go home."

"Suits me fine. I would love to spend more time with you," he said, brushing her cheek with his lips. "I'm excited to explore the beauty of my homeland with you and have the opportunity to show you what you mean to me."

"I'm there for all of that," she said, with a mischievous grin that made him want to abandon the party for a rendezvous of their own.

All in good time.

Rashid slipped an arm around the woman who was destined to be part of his future. Grateful that Imad's plan hadn't succeeded.

He vowed in his heart to always give his all to keep her safe and not allow people to abuse her gift.

Writing and Chaos

Happen. Our job is to always give fuel to keep the fire and not allow people to blow it out.[?]

Chapter 20

The room suddenly vibrated with power that felt like jolts of electricity, causing Yolanda to scan the area. She suddenly felt light-headed and her body trembled. Warmth surged through her veins as if someone had turned up the heat. Yolanda searched the crowd look for Martina Rossi, fearing that she might need some healing. Everything in the room was doubled and wavy. Her chest muscles tighten up.

"Who are you looking for?" Rashid touched her shoulder as one of the waitstaff approached with a tray of appetizers.

"Martina. I was hoping she'd show up despite originally turning down the invitation." She shrugged, not sure what was going on with her but glad the weird feelings had started to fade.

A couple stopped in front of them, lifting miniature shawarma pitas as Rashid leaned closer to her ear. "She's putting out fires at home. Based on the conversation I overheard, her past is challenging her current lifestyle."

"I sense she had a dark secret." Yolanda pulled out her phone and glanced at it, making sure it was off. Gratefully, the weird feeling was going away. "I was hoping that she'd open up a little more in person than she had on our video chats."

"It will all be revealed in time." Rashid guided her through the people milling about. "Possibly when you return to Chicago."

She stepped out onto the balcony. "Umm. With Imad trying to kill you, I've had enough excitement for a while. So, I won't pursue answers, but if she needs me…."

"You are there." Rashid smiled.

"That experience was scary for everyone involved." He grabbed both of her hands. "Thank you again for what you have done."

Yolanda felt a surge of emotion engulf her like a warm hug. "I appreciate you for making sure I received the best treatment. The kabillion flowers were overkill though." She stared into his eyes. He had tracked down her aunt when her mother had been unable to heal her. Her mother's gift was not healing. but he had not known that until her parents had arrived. "Were you behind Sheikh Kamran asking me to be on a special task force?"

"Maybe." He pulled her into an embrace, kissing her forehead. "Am I wrong to want you to stay here so I can keep an eye on you?"

Angela approached. "Sorry to interrupt, but Khalil and Kamran would like a word with you."

They followed her through the crowd into a private room. Khalil, Sheikh Kamran and a woman Yolanda never seen before were in the room.

"I'll be outside." Angela closed the door behind them.

"Rashid. Yolanda. This is Jalisa." Sheikh Kamaran motioned to the woman with strawberry blonde hair and grey eyes.

Rashid shook her hand, but Yolanda hesitated. She had never met a person with a rainbow aura. Jalisa took Yolanda's hand and the world went still. She could see a large portal between the Castle in Wilmette and the Palace in Durabia. People emerged from the mist and some from the ground. Yolanda ripped her hand away as a powerful surge went through her body.

"Are you okay?" Rashid whispered in her ear.

Yolanda nodded, but she wasn't sure.

"Congratulations on winning this round," Jalisa said, focusing on Yolanda. "I'm honored to have you and Rashid as a part of the task force."

"You have crippled the Fades." Khalil explained the ongoing battle between the Tala and Fades since their ship crashed to earth. Part of the ship lies under the Durabian Palace and the Castle in Wilmette. The Fades want to annihilate the Tala so that they could strip the world of its resources.

Sheikh Kamran motioned for them to sit down. "They have to find a new way to finance their plan."

"All I did was heal Rashid." Yolanda felt uncomfortable with the praise she didn't deserve.

"If you hadn't," Sheikh Kamran looked at his nephew. "They would have succeeded in funding their plan to take over the Palace."

"I know you realize every healer is not like you." Jalisa moved closer to Yolanda.

Yolanda felt her chest tighten. Were they telling her she was a Tala? Are Sheikh Kamran, Khalil, Rashid and her parents not of this world? Had the Busch family been Fades? Will Fades come after her? She tried to keep her face neutral even though mentally she was freaking out.

"Most humans don't tap into their gifts." Jalisa looked between her and Rashid.

Her shoulders dropped with relief knowing that she was not Tala. Her mind was already trying to wrap itself around Talas and Fades walking among them. To have found out she was from another planet would have been too much to handle. She had so many questions. How had Khalil and Kamran come to know about them? Does Daron's team know? How can they tell a Tala from a Fade? If they attacked, can they be killed? Why didn't the Tala intervene before things got bad?

Breathe, Yolanda. You'll get all those answers in good time.

"Everyone on the team will not be aware that some of the evil we will battle is otherworldly." Khalil turned and pointed towards the wall that now had a picture of five women: Bethany Scott, Martina Rossi, Audrey "Deuce" Meadows, Maxine Ferguson and Mia Ferguson with three black boxes that just said guardian one, two and three. "These are the people who will understand about the Tala and Fade."

Yolanda wondered if Jalisa was one of the guardians since neither Khalil nor Sheikh Kamran had explained her presence in the room. She wondered if the women on the wall were Tala or gifted humans.

You're special but your gift is evolving, Jalisa said.

"In what ways?" Yolanda not knowing if she liked the sound of that. Rashid looked at her with confusion etched on his face, making her realize that Jalisa hadn't spoken the words out loud.

Jalisa gave her a gentle smile. "Only time will tell, but for now. Be proud of what you did and who you are."

Khalil took one of Yolanda's hands and one of Rashid's. "As your relationship grows, remember the two of you are stronger together."

She glanced at Rashid with happiness in her heart that he was the man turning her aura red. Her aunt had confirmed what she had once feared. That it would only happen when she met her intended mate. Since his aura wasn't red, but hers changed, it was a strong indicator that he was a love match.

Khalil released their hands. "Are you willing to step up if needed in the future?"

"Yes." Rashid squeezed Yolanda's hand.

Sheikh Kamran, Jalisa and Khalil all stared at Yolanda awaiting her response.

"Without question, even if my knees are knocking and my hands are shaking." Yolanda realized that she didn't want to be on the sidelines of the war between good and evil. She promised herself to learn more about her gift, the Tala and Fade, and her connection to Rashid. If the war came in her lifetime, she wanted to be ready.

The Reckoning

Chapter 1

A pair of hands traced Martina's body, caressed every curve, causing her to squirm with delight. Heat ignited as her lover teased those pleasure zones, working her into a frenzy.

Moments later, cold air replaced the sensual warmth. Those same hands bringing satisfaction were now wrapped firmly around her slender neck. Black blossoms of death bloomed at the corners of her eyes. Life and death existed beneath his grip. He hauled her closer, breathing her in like a fine wine.

"How quaint. A Healer that can't heal thyself. I could smell you from miles away. The energy you give off is better than blood." The guttural laugh rolled in his chest like thunder as his forked tongue slithered between razor-sharp teeth. It trailed across the skin at her collarbone and blistered.

"Help, please help me," she screamed in her head. All she could do was look into the eyes of her betrayer as life ebbed from her body.

"Do you have any idea what lies beneath the floorboards of this castle?" he asked as his eyes glittered with a mixture of love and hate that bordered on madness. Reptilian lids blinked over horizontal pupils that shrank down to murderous slits. "So close to the source and yet so far. You reek of humanity."

Bolting straight up in bed, her eyelids snapped open. Thoughts were in a haze while sweat pooled in her armpits and ran down her forehead.

She fought to get out from under the blanket while trying to figure out why this dream seemed so real. Did last night's events have something to do with it? Past fears resurfacing? Martina hissed as her fingers found a neat row of blisters. It wasn't the first time one of the Fades had found her, and it wouldn't be the last.

The life that she led before the Castle was one filled with unimaginable acts. It was a mix of ending and saving lives. A web of duplicity that was masterfully woven.

Martina lay in the darkness of her master bedroom, trying to get her bearings. Eerie silence filled the space. Daylight tried to peek in, but the blackout drapery engulfed her in blackness. She sat up slowly, scanning the room while her pupils adjusted, and she put a warm hand over the blisters and winced in pain as the heat intensified, drawing the venom from her body before the liquid crept into her veins and sent the blue poison crawling through her face like fire ants in a frenzy. They always sent an ambassador when she got too close. Running wasn't an option. She would stand shoulder to shoulder with the others, just as her predecessors did. To do anything less was a betrayal of the worst kind; one she, and perhaps even the world, would never recover from.

Closing her eyes for a few seconds, a vision of the man she loved filled her mind. Martina took deep breaths to calm her racing heart as she recalled their time together last night.

Shrimp carbonara, garlic bread, Moscato d'Asti, and Tiramisu were served during the private dinner in her lover's suite. They feasted on the delicious, mouth-watering Italian cuisine while smooth jazz played in the background.

He reached for her hand, pulling her in for a slow, seductive dance to the soothing sounds. Her head briefly lay on his firm chest. He had an athletic build and stood six feet tall.

Martina gazed into his dark brown eyes, mesmerized by the wanton look in them. He lowered his head to kiss her, and she ran her hands through his cropped, salt-and-pepper hair. Their tongues tangled, kissing as if they were trying to devour one another. After coming up for air, he led her into the master bedroom.

In the depths of her core, she still felt the carnal, uninhibited actions of last night. Spine-tingling, toe-curling, back-scratching rawness. He filled her and feasted until she overflowed. The man was relentless and worked her body into exhaustion.

No other man came close to possessing every fiber of Martina's being. Pure ecstasy, then utter chaos. The peaceful mood shifted to a hostile environment, replacing their naked embrace.

Tempers got the best of them, and their argument escalated quickly. One honest question turned a satisfying evening into the scene of a contentious standoff.

"It's a simple question. What are we, and why are we keeping our relationship a secret?" She snapped. "It's not like people haven't seen us together."

"Martina, we've talked about this," he replied in an exasperated tone. We must be careful until the deal is completed. Just because people have seen us together doesn't mean that they deserve confirmation."

"I couldn't care less about business right now. I'm more concerned about how you truly feel about me and this relationship."

"You know I care deeply about you. Otherwise, you wouldn't be here or in my life."

"You care deeply about me?" she taunted, scorching him with a fiery glance. "So what are we? Friends with benefits? Something to do? What?"

His gaze raked over her. "I meant precisely what I said. I care deeply about you. Did I say something wrong?"

Without a word or warning, Martina grabbed the clothes she had tossed all over the floor on her side of the bed. She wanted more - marriage and children of her own.

"What are you doing, amore mio?" he asked in a voice too calm for the moment.

Silence.

With athletic agility, he rose from the bed and grabbed her arms to halt any movement. Turning her body towards his, he removed the clothes from her hands, throwing them back to the floor without breaking eye contact.

Martina breathed heavily while trying to loosen his grip, but couldn't.

"I'm not letting you go in this mood," he said through his teeth.

Without warning, he ravished her lips, forcing her mouth open and coiling his tongue around hers until the tension evaporated from her body. He looked into her eyes. "I'm not done with you yet."

"You don't control me, stronzo." She allowed the insult to roll off her tongue, flavored with spite. "You may not be done with me, but I'm certainly done with you."

His eyes held a twinkle of mischief as he laughed. "I'm going to show you again what this *asshole* can do." He pulled her against his body, kissing her until she was breathless. Seconds later, all the momentary tension vanished from the room.

No other words were spoken, and she allowed him to have his way with her. One touch from this man rendered Martina powerless every time. Her mind, body, and heart were constantly at odds with one another when it came to him. Leonardo Salvatore was the one person who clenched her heart in his hands. The puppet master controlling the strings.

An hour later, after making sure he was asleep for the night, she dressed and retired to her private suite. Little did he know that the argument was not over. He won this round, but not the war. Leonardo had his part to play in the endgame. Dead or alive, she was there to ensure he completed the task.

Kings of the Castle

Burning this place to the ground would be a kindness." Khalil Germaine's steps faltered for a moment, and his hands curled into fists by his side. "We should have known better. *I* should have known better."

Vikkas glanced at his father. Deep lines edged the older man's mouth, chiseled by grief and regret. "Don't say that. None of what happened here is your fault."

"Of course it is," Khalil shot back as a gust of air from the cooling system blew the tunic around his muscular form. "I built this place with my own hands. I am the one who entrusted them with my legacy for five years."

"You couldn't have known what they would do."

Khalil released a weary sigh that spoke volumes to his inner turmoil. "Wealth invites greed, and absolute power corrupts even those with the best of intentions. Every student of history knows as much—I taught you those lessons myself. I taught the other eight as well."

"That's true," Vikkas conceded, falling in step with his father as they trailed the length of the hidden passage, undetected. "But not all men are weak. You taught me that, too. Wealth and power never changed your heart."

Khalil's arm chopped through the air, dismissing his words with an angry wave. "But now my heart has come to nothing."

Before Vikkas could protest, his father veered toward the massive wall.

Vikkas shifted his weight onto the balls of his feet as nervous energy snaked up his spine. "Are you sure breaking into The Castle is a good idea? They killed Zahara, just for warning us. We should wait for the others."

"We cannot afford to wait. Her death must not be in vain." Khalil choked on the words as his fingertips slid over the cool stone as though marking their progression. "They will not give up their power so easily. By tomorrow, everything she died for could vanish."

"But the evidence—the dossiers and photos. What they did to those women … to the *children* … they can't explain all that away."

Khalil paused to look at Vikkas over his shoulder. "You live in a civilized world. For that, I am grateful. But you have no idea what lies beneath. The corruption that protects men of privilege runs deep—far deeper than you know."

Vikkas thought of the journal that an original Castle member had sent to their hotel room, the one that contained pages of entries that detailed all the damage that had been done. One entry in particular had aged his father nearly ten years and chilled his own blood …

Delivered a prepubescent female submissive…trained to serve wherever and however needed. Bonus: Vocal cords are severed to ensure discretion.

And this was the mildest of the crimes that had been committed.

Vikkas frowned. "I'm not a child. Or a fool."

His father twisted far enough to clap a conciliatory hand on his shoulder. "Of course not. You are a man of principle; I am proud of that. But it also blinds you. All of you. Which is why you will need each other."

"Who?" He met his father's gaze with a mix of curiosity and

annoyance. "Why these eight men? And why haven't they answered?"

"They will." For the first time that night, Khalil smiled. "They are bold, like you, especially when it comes to protecting the ones they love—shoot first, ask questions never." He took in a breath that seemed ladened with bitterness and regret. "They are still finding pieces of Zahara like flower petals cast upon an ocean of sorrow and shame. Her only crime was speaking with me about the terrible things she witnessed at the Castle."

Vikkas turned back to the wall as Khalil whispered, "The underworld came running the moment we left the States. Now you, and those eight men I summoned, are the key to The Castle's redemption. They. Will. Make. Things. Right." He locked gazes with Vikkas and added, "But to avoid unnecessary bloodshed, they should not see us—or them—coming."

Vikkas tensed and moved closer to the wall. When nothing happened, he blew a hard breath from his lips. "Is this the right place?"

"Yes. Help me." Khalil pointed to the area that had nine faint scratches on the surface. "Right here."

Khalil regarded his son in patient silence.

"Where, here?" He pressed his hands against the stone.

He nodded. "Just so. Push."

Vikkas did as his father asked. At first, he felt only the expected, perfect resistance of an impenetrable stone wall, but then something shifted. He shoved harder, and the stone gave way beneath his hands. They stepped into the night air. Someone laughed, and their progression halted. Vikkas' head swiveled in the direction of the sound. Several armed men had chosen their exit point for a smoke break.

"We have to go back to the conference room and exit through the front." His heart quickened as he quickly ushered his father back inside.

"This passage also leads to a camera blind spot on the main

level." Khalil headed in the opposite direction of the conference room.

Vikkas waited until the hidden door closed, sent off a text to their driver, and followed his father. Seconds later, his phone vibrated. "The car should be here by the time we make it to the driveway," he whispered.

Khalil cracked open the exit slightly and peered out into the main level corridor. "The hallway is clear."

They stepped out but didn't start moving until the hidden entrance closed, then walked to the front doors. Vikkas scanned the lengthy golden entrance with three red strips of carpet, two of which went up a double set of stairs and the other down the hallway in the center. Two vases filled with artfully arranged flowers on the sideboards were on either side of the opening. A long dark polished wood table used to register Castle guests, sat in the area between the foyer and the grand staircases. They were waiting in the hallway not too far from the table.

As they neared the exit, Vikkas patted his pocket and felt for the flash drive with the evidence that would set things in motion. He muttered another curse. "I left my wallet in the conference room." He had retrieved the safe's access card from it then sat it on the conference table. Vikkas couldn't leave it behind with that and their hotel keycard in it. "I'll be back."

"Be quick about it."

Vikkas pivoted, took a few hurried steps, and noticed a red light blinking rapidly as he came closer. He turned to ask his father if he'd seen it when a shadow flickered, and Khalil lunged at it.

An ambush. They were waiting for us.

That was all Vikkas had time to think before instinct took over and he bolted in their direction.

A movement to the left caught his attention moments before a massive man rushed toward him. The goon reached for a holster beneath his grey suit jacket.

Vikkas reached the registration table in two quick strides,

throwing his palm down to vault himself over the table, and launching his feet toward the giant. Two large men, both armed coming for them, and his father didn't have the speed he once had. If he didn't take them both out quickly—

Don't think. Just fight.

His boots connected with the man's chest and knocked him to the ground. Vikkas had hoped the impact would dislodge the weapon from his hand, but the goon had an iron grip. Without even trying to get up, the man raised the gun and fired as Vikkas fell on him. A searing pain blazed across Vikkas' arm.

Vikkas grabbed grey suit's wrist, shoving the barrel away as the man fired off a barrage of rounds in an ear-ringing staccato. Where was his father? Was he hit? Adrenaline surged through him, and Vikkas pummeled the man in the face as hard and fast as he could.

Three punches. Four. Five. As his fist connected for the sixth time, slick, fresh blood coated his knuckles. Several more rounds went off. After the last one, Vikkas saw the man's bloody teeth glistening through a wide gap that had opened between his lip and chin. With the seventh punch, the gun finally slid away, clattering across the floor and disappearing from view as the man threw up his hands, trying to save what was left of his face.

His plan had been to grab the pistol as soon as the guy let go. But now he had no time to find where it had landed.

Not seeing the weapon nearby, Vikkas rose and issued a kick to the man's chest that knocked the wind out of him. He spotted grey suit's firearm and spun in one fluid motion, flying over the table again.

Another gun went off, and his stomach turned to ice. But no, his father was still on his feet, locked in a struggle with the other man, trying to keep his arm pointed away from Vikkas. The pistol swung back in his direction, and Khalil slammed his elbow down into the man's arm. The gun went off again, and the bullet smashed into the floor. Vikkas shifted gears, realizing going for grey suit's weapon would put him in the other goon's line of fire.

As grey suit struggled to his feet, Vikkas raced to a sideboard table, and snatched up the closest vase—a solid marble bludgeon that fit perfectly in his hand. His father was still struggling with his assailant, and then Vikkas was staring straight down the barrel of a Glock.

Grey suit must have had a second gun.

Without hesitation, he slammed the vase across the giant's head like a bat. The man hit the ground with a solid thud. He gave one last punch for good measure and was satisfied when the man's head rolled to the side, arms fell to the ground and eyes fluttered to a close.

Khalil wrestled for the weapon with a man dressed in black. Vikkas didn't wait to see who won that battle. He spun in their direction and raced toward them. Khalil tripped over the carpet's edge and gave the intruder an advantage.

When the pistol fired several shots, Vikkas couldn't see the flash. Had his father had taken the hit?

A split second later, he reached "black suit" and fell on him in a fury. Vikkas slammed the vase into his head, over and over. On the third hit, he felt the gunman's cheek give way, crushed beneath the force of his rage. With a fourth swing, the man raised his arms blindly in front of him, trying to block the blow. The crack of an upper forearm was unmistakable even over the newcomer's shouts for them to leave. The man screamed, dropped his gun, and ran out the front door, cradling his misshapen limb.

Vikkas scooped up the pistol and spun around, still brandishing the vase in one hand as he leveled the gun at the giant in the grey suit who ran up on them. He pulled the trigger, but the weapon only clicked. *Must've been damaged by the vase.*

The beast of a man stared at him, a slow, bloody grin spreading across his face. He raised the gun and aimed at his father.

Vikkas lunged in front of Khalil just before the beast fired.

Click.

He was out of ammo. Vikkas grinned back. Dropping the gun,

he snatched up the second vase, launched himself at him, yelling like a maniac and waving the vase through the air.

The big guy wasn't having any part of it. With a look of raw terror, he turned tail and ran.

Father.

Vikkas scrambled to Khalil with his arm throbbing and bleeding, taking in the blood darkening the front of his father's tunic. He fell to his knees and tore the cloth apart to assess the damage. At the very least, the bullet had punctured a lung. *Had it hit his heart?* He applied pressure to the wound with one hand and snatched his phone from his pocket with the other.

Before he could make the call, running footsteps echoed behind him. He whipped his head around, about to reach for the vase, but then he saw who it was.

"I called for help. An ambulance is on the way."

"Some help you were," Vikkas growled, realizing the man had been there long enough to provide some assistance besides dialing a number.

"Stop." The command came from Khalil, his voice thready yet firm. "Protect him. He cannot be caught up in this."

"Protect him?" Vikkas huffed. "Dispatch will see the number on *their* end."

"It's a burner phone."

"Stay back." Vikkas lifted his bloody palm to warn off the interloper.

"What the hell happened?" he asked, instead of doing as he was commanded.

"Leave." He tightened his hold on his father. "Before the authorities arrive."

The man stared at the spreading stain on Khalil's tunic, his feet planted on the ground.

Vikkas swallowed hard and calmed the fear raging inside him. "No one can know you were here." He nodded toward the front door that still stood open to the night, indicating the nearby parking lot and its fleet of luxury cars. The wailing sirens blasted in a way that signaled the first responders were close. "Go. Help is on the way."

Finally, the man turned away, walking then running out the front doors.

Khalil groaned, watching Vikkas through half-closed lids. "Remember the mission. They *will* come. Tell them this: 'Evil prevails when good men do nothing.' They *are* good men, my son. The absolute best. They will come. They must. The Castle belongs to ..."

His father's eyes closed, his skin turning gray, and Vikkas's heart threatened to burst from his chest. He maintained pressure on the wound, wishing he had more hands—or his own life to give.

"Father." He spoke the word through clenched teeth, barely trusting his voice. "Don't you dare die on me."

Transition of Power

Cameron Stone sat in a black Dodge Charger looking at her parents' house. She took a moment to prepare herself before she entered the three-story, blonde brick building with white trim around the windows. Visiting her mother, sometimes put Cameron in an odd place. She had battled men three times her size, conversed with some of the most intelligent people around the globe, yet she couldn't deal with her 5'2" mother on certain days. Her mother, ever the campaigner, always tried to do one of three things—mend fences, make a lady out of Cameron, or marry her off. She hadn't been successful at any of the three.

Cameron tightened the black bandana over her braided hair before sliding out of the driver's seat. She didn't plan to stay long because it was too close to dinner time and she had no intention of being there when her father arrived. Since the incident that led her down the not-so-straight and narrow path of the underworld of Chicago, she had only laid eyes on him a few times.

The light oak door opened as she climbed the concrete stairs. *What the hell was he doing there?* Cameron fumed as the youngest of her brothers stepped outside. She selected today to visit because her mother was supposed to be alone.

She scowled, taking in the tawny skin that was so much like their father's. Her brother, Jason, was several inches taller than her. "Didn't know you'd be here."

"Or what?" Jason snapped, face morphing into a frown that matched her own. "You wouldn't have come?"

"Pretty much." Cameron crossed her arms over her chest. "I'm not in the mood for your legendary lip service or lectures."

If Justin and Jaime Quinn were also present, she'd definitely leave and come back another day. She stared at Jason, knowing the days of getting back the brother who once knew all her secrets were long gone. In his place was "daddy junior" with his father's judgmental expressions, searing stares, and his knack for being an authority on everything.

"The lifestyle you're living isn't right," Jason scolded, his hazel eyes squinting and his nose crinkled as though he smelled something rotten.

"As I remember, my brothers introduced me to my current lifestyle." The last thing Cameron wanted to do was rehash a painful past but she also wouldn't let him forget his role in her current situation.

Jason leaned in the doorway, blocking her path. "Yeah, but *we* got out. What's your excuse?"

Cameron tried unsuccessfully to keep the anger out her voice as she moved back. "If memory serves me right, your *father* got you out."

"He's your father, too," he countered, pulling the silver doorknob forward and stepping further onto the porch. Cars swished by on the street behind them.

"Technically, he's my sperm donor." She sighed, hating this bickering session that occurred every time they were within a few feet of each other. She'd once considered herself, Jason, and their cousin, JD, like a three-cord rope, hard to break apart. "Tell Mom I'll stop by to see her another time."

"Jason, is that Cookie?" their mother's soft voice called from beyond the door.

"Yeah, it's her," Jason answered dryly.

"Then let her in." She ambled from the hallway and pushed Jason out of the way. "How's my baby girl doing? Not good, seeing those dimples have disappeared."

"I'm fine." Her family claimed her dimples vanished whenever she was angry. Cameron gave Jason the evil eye as she slid past him into the house. If Jason wasn't standing there, Caroline Stone would have said something about Cameron's black jeans and baggy sweat-shirt not being feminine enough. She would be right.

Cameron had her mom's light, barely-there complexion and oval face, but her curvy shape was a replica of her Aunt Renee's infamous one. Her height came from the other side of the DNA strand. Each of her brothers' square faces, varying shades of tawny brown skin and hazel eyes were their father's contribution. The rest of their features had a strong resemblance of their mother's African-Native American side of the family.

Lavender perfume tickled Cameron's nose as Caroline's arms wrapped about Cameron's waist, then the petite woman pushed her toward a rose-gold couch. "I was telling your brother that your Aunt Renee was worried about JD."

Jason frowned as Cameron claimed a seat next to their mother. "I'm looking into it."

"I'm trying to catch up with him, too," Cameron said, ignoring Jason who loomed over her, as though wishing he could put a muzzle on her.

"She'll be glad to hear that," Caroline said as the phone rang. "Let me get that."

Caroline hustled toward the kitchen. The only people who called the house phone were church folks and older family members. It had taken forever to get Caroline Stone used to a cell phone.

Jason waited until their mother was in a full-blown conversation before growling, "Cam, don't get involved."

She chuckled, since she had no idea what he meant. "In what?"

"JD's back in trouble," Jason whispered, glancing at their mother who was still in an animated conversation which wasn't a good sign given her body language.

Cameron rose, put a hand on her chest and schooled her expression into a more innocent one. "I didn't—"

"He's safe for now but don't interfere. Trust me," he said in a low, almost raspy timbre.

"Trust you," Cameron snapped, shoving his shoulder and daring him to do something. "Six of us were there that night when you were shown the error of your wicked ways. You, Que, and your two friends were redeemed, and JD and I were not. Trusting you is not an option."

The Stone clan had grown up in the south suburbs of Chicago and would sometimes catch the train into the city. When Quinn and Jason found a new set of friends, the trips became more adventurous. What started as a dare to shoplift small items from department stores without getting caught, then spiraled into procuring high-end merchandise.

"It wasn't my choice to leave you behind bars," Jason argued, adopting a wide stance with his chin jutted out.

"No, it was your *father's* choice," she countered, glaring at him. "You accepted it. Reaped the benefits. Now, you want me to trust you." She tried not to relive the shock and betrayal of Jake Stone getting Quinn and Jason and their friends out of jail and leaving Cameron and JD in that cell as though they didn't matter. Her brothers didn't even attempt to reach out to her after "the incident." Therein lay the separation of the black sheep from the flock.

"JD's life may depend on it." Jason angled himself so he had a better view of the kitchen. "I know what's going on and it's being handled. FBI's all over it."

All of her brothers had followed in her father's footsteps, embracing some form of law enforcement. She, on the other hand, found herself entangled in the darkness and shadow of the criminal world. Despite his assertions, she didn't trust any of them to do right by JD. "Then let's work together," Cameron suggested.

"Our cousin needs to find a job that doesn't have ties to organized crime and stop dragging you into his mess."

"I can't sit idle while you all try to figure it out," she shot back.

Cameron scowled more, not wanting to let Jason know his words hit home. Both JD and her lives would be different had JD had the confidence to fight for his dream of being an artist when he was young. Unfortunately, his friends convinced him that his artwork was trash and would never make real money. Then they introduced him to Bishop, who could make them all wealthy men and JD went to work for him. Nothing was the same after that.

"Let the proper authorities handle it." He shifted his gaze toward the sound of their mother's laughter. "I'm serious, Cam. Leave it alone."

Cameron edged forward until mere inches remained between them. "Don't you wish I would."

"More than JD's life is on the line here," he shot back. "If I find out you're in the way, I'll arrest you in a heartbeat." Jason stared her down, daring her to defy him. He retreated a few feet as their mother's head peeked out from around the dining room wall that had finally been painted in that eggshell color their father hated. She'd finally won that tug-of-war that had been going on for at least three years.

Cameron balled her fist and silently counted to ten. "You would, wouldn't you? Like father, like son."

Jason frowned with an air of dismissiveness, something that also made him more like his father. "Don't start that."

"I'm saying bye to mom. I'll see you around." She walked over to the pint-sized woman, kissed her moist cheek, and whispered a farewell.

"Cameron," he called after her, but she ignored him.

Her mother covered the mouthpiece and whispered, "See you tomorrow?"

Cameron gave a noncommittal shrug, then shifted her focus into the living room in time to see Jason blocking the path to the door. She was tempted to leave out the back way but all he'd do was slide out the front and plant his behind on her Charger.

"Bye, Jason." She brushed past him, knocking into his shoulder, then grabbed the knob, swinging the door open. As Cameron attempted to close the door, Jason caught it.

He trotted to catch up as she raced to the curb. "The best I can do is update you on JD's status."

Realization hit her. Jason not only knew where JD was, but who he was with. "You've got eyes in the organization." She was so angry she hadn't been listening to what he wasn't saying.

"I can't comment on that." Jason's face went blank, same as when his father caught them doing something they weren't supposed to do. They all knew anything said could be twisted, turned, and used against them.

Cameron deactivated the locks on her vehicle. "You don't have to bother, brother dear." She slid behind the wheel and pulled away, leaving her frustrated brother standing on the curb.

Karen's Bio

National bestselling author, Karen D. Bradley, has penned several contemporary fiction, suspense, psychological thrillers, and romantic suspense. She has also contributed short stories to the Sugar anthology and the Just One Kiss anthology. Venturing into film making, she wrote and produced a short film based on one of her novels.

Visit Karen on the web at www.karendbradley.com

Join her mailing list: https://landing.mailerlite.com/webforms/landing/p2l5h5

Karen's Bio

Kings of the Castle Series

USA TODAY and New York Times Bestselling Authors work together to provide you with a world you'll never want to leave. It's time to discover *The Castle*.

Fate made them brothers. Protecting the Castle, each other, and the women they love will make them Kings.

Each King book 2-9 is a standalone, NO cliffhangers

Book 1 – Kings of the Castle, the introduction to the series and story of King of Wilmette (Vikkas Germaine)

USA TODAY, *New York Times*, and National Bestselling Authors work together to provide you with a world you'll never want to leave. The Castle.

Fate made them brothers, but protecting the Castle, each other, and the women they love, will make them Kings. Their combined efforts to find the current Castle members responsible for the attempt on their mentor's life, is the beginning of dangerous challenges that will alter the path of their lives forever.

These powerful men, unexpectedly brought together by their pasts and current circumstances, will become a force to be reckoned with.

King of Chatham - Book 2 – London St. Charles

While Mariano "Reno" DeLuca uses his skills and resources to create safe havens for battered women, a surge in criminal activity within the Chatham area threatens the women's anonymity and security. When Zuri, an exotic Tanzanian Princess, arrives seeking refuge from an arranged marriage and its deadly consequences, Reno is now forced to relocate the women in the shelter, fend off unforeseen enemies of The Castle, and endeavor not to lose his heart to the mysterious woman.

King of Evanston - Book 3 - J. L. Campbell

Raised as an immigrant, he knows the heartache of family separation firsthand. His personal goals and business ethics collide when a vulnerable woman stands to lose her baby in an under-handed and profitable scheme crafted by powerful, ruthless businessmen and politicians who have nefarious ties to The Castle. Shaz and the Kings of the Castle collaborate to uproot the dark forces intent on changing the balance of power within The Castle and destroying their mentor. National Bestselling Author, J.L. Campbell presents book 3 in the Kings of the Castle Series, featuring Shaz Bostwick.

King of Devon - Book 4 - Naleighna Kai

When a coma patient becomes pregnant, Jaidev Maharaj's medical facility comes under a government microscope and media scrutiny. In the midst of the investigation, he receives a mysterious call from someone in his past that demands that more of him than he's ever been willing to give and is made aware of a dark family secret that will destroy the people he loves most.

King of Morgan Park - Book 5 - Karen D. Bradley

Two things threaten to destroy several areas of Daron Kincaid's life —the tracking device he developed to locate victims of sex trafficking and an inherited membership in a mysterious outfit called The Castle. The new developments set the stage to dismantle the relationship with a woman who's been trained to make men weak or put them on the other side of the grave. The secrets Daron keeps from Cameron and his inner circle only complicates an already tumultuous situation caused by an FBI sting that brought down his former enemies. Can Daron take on his enemies, manage his secrets and loyalty to the Castle without permanently losing the woman he loves?

King of South Shore - Book 6 - MarZe Scott

Award-winning real estate developer, Kaleb Valentine, is known for turning failing communities into thriving havens in the Metro Detroit area. His plans to rebuild his hometown neighborhood are dereailed with one phone call that puts Kaleb deep in the middle of an intense criminal investigation led by a detective who has a personal vendetta. Now he will have to deal with the ghosts of his past before they kill him.

King of Lincoln Park - Book 7 – Martha Kennerson

Grant Khambrel is a sexy, successful architect with big plans to expand his Texas Company. Unfortunately, a dark secret from his past could destroy it all unless he's willing to betray the man responsible for that success, and the woman who becomes the key to his salvation.

King of Hyde Park - Book 8 -Lisa Dodson

Alejandro "Dro" Reyes has been a "fixer" for as long as he could remember, which makes owning a crisis management company focused on repairing professional reputations the perfect fit. The same could be said of Lola Samuels, who is only vaguely aware of his "true" talents and seems to be oblivious to the growing attraction between them. His company, Vantage Point, is in high demand and business in the Windy City is booming. Until a mysterious call following an attempt on his mentor's life forces him to drop every-thing and accept a fated position with The Castle. But there's a hidden agenda and unexpected enemy that Alejandro doesn't see coming who threatens his life, his woman, and his throne.

King of Lawndale - Book 9 - Janice M. Allen

Dwayne Harper's passion is giving disadvantaged boys the tools to transform themselves into successful men. Unfortunately, the minute he steps up to take his place among the men he considers brothers, two things stand in his way: a political office that does not want the competition Dwayne's new education system will bring, and a well-connected former member of The Castle who will use everything in his power—even those who Dwayne mentors—to shut him down.

Don't miss the hot new standalone series. The Kings of the Castle made them family, but the Knights will transform the world.

www.ingramcontent.com/pod-product-compliance
Lightning Source LLC
Chambersburg PA
CBHW011425200626
46814CB00017B/3009